T0355013

GEMINI

JIMMY TAAFFE

ARCHWAY
PUBLISHING

Archway Publishing books may be ordered through booksellers or by contacting:

Archway Publishing
1663 Liberty Drive
Bloomington, IN 47403
www.archwaypublishing.com
844-669-3957

ISBN: 978-1-6657-2379-4 (sc)
ISBN: 978-1-6657-2381-7 (hc)
ISBN: 978-1-6657-2380-0 (e)

Library of Congress Control Number: 2022909128

Print information available on the last page.

Archway Publishing rev. date: 05/10/2022

Prologue

The Nepalese Sherpa craned his neck upward as the fireball streaked across the eastern sky, lighting up the peaks of the snowy mountaintops like the flash from a camera. He watched as the perfectly round ball flung strings and beads of blue and red liquid light in all directions. His mouth fell agape as his eyes followed the fiery orb across the afternoon sky.

"The hand of God!" the weathered Sherpa whispered in a puff of frosty breath.

In an instant, the orb disappeared over the peaks, and the cold day reset itself. The Sherpa fell to his knees and continued to gaze skyward into the heavens. Moments later, he lifted himself with a grunt and began to walk the final miles to his village, constantly looking skyward as he walked across the barren snow fields.

Fifteen years later, as the Sherpa lay dying on his thin, tattered mattress, he would recount for the first time what he had seen in the sky that day. His eldest son, Akash, listened to his father obediently and with patience. Modern influences had permeated their small village, and such things as lights that seemed to dance in the mountains, spirits that floated across the ice fields, and the existence of the yeti were seen as simple folklore in the modern age. Akash dismissed his father's stories and softly kissed his forehead.

"Rest, Papa," he said with a sad smile.

Unbeknownst to the dying Sherpa and his son, the craft he had seen years ago in the sky carried one lone occupant: a single Gemini, searching for the other.

BOOK ONE

1

Josi. The Men in Black. Star Whisperer

JOSI ANDOLINI WAS JUST TWENTY-TWO YEARS old when she started her first teaching job at PS 51 in the Hell's Kitchen neighborhood in Manhattan, New York. Immediately after high school, she enrolled at Lander College, and three and a half years later, she graduated summa cum laude with her degree in education. She immediately went to work at her alma mater. Surprisingly, education was not her first choice, but it seemed to be her best choice at the time. Ever since she could remember, she had loved art, science, and history. She knew she could channel her love of these subjects into something somewhat meaningful and purposeful with teaching.

Even at the young and still tender age of twenty-two, Josi felt like a spinster of sorts. She rarely, if ever, dated and was more than content spending her weekends alone in her little and meticulously kept apartment on 44th Street in Hell's Kitchen. Most of her evenings were spent grading papers and watching the myriad of shows she had discovered on Netflix. She read with hyperactive enthusiasm and became a casual expert in a great many areas.

She had cultivated a rather strange obsession with the game of baseball. She loved the sport on so many levels—from its rich and vibrant history to its indulgence of numbers and statistics. Most Saturdays during the season, she would ride the D train to Yankee Stadium and sit in the bleachers with her scorecard on her lap and the tip of her pencil in the corner of her mouth. Her eyes would dart back and forth behind her huge, designer-knockoff sunglasses. On Saturdays when her Yanks were on the road, she would visit flea markets in Brooklyn and the Bronx, looking for odd and interesting books about baseball.

She had a very small but loyal group of friends she could count on. Most of them were slightly older and had already embarked on their journey filled with husbands, children, and careers. Secretly, Josi felt a tinge of sympathy toward them. Something deep in her inner pool of logic told her that they may not be as happy as they led on when they dished about their perfect lives at dinner parties and Christmas Eve celebrations.

It certainly was not at all uncommon for her to have interested gentleman callers of her own. A great many suitors had swooned over her in the last few years, and Josi generally, in the politest terms she could come up with, passed on their advances. She supposed they thought she might be a lesbian, or parvenu-like, but that was not the case. Her internal system of social hardwiring just meant she functioned slightly differently than most people. She felt absolutely no real maternal drive and no instinctive matronly longing to push her to find a man. She lived her life in a semi-self-imposed bubble, and that was just fine with her. She seemed to always be in a constant state of flux, always knowing in the deep recesses of her mind that a great change might be at hand.

Her grandmother would call her "bewitchingly angelic"—a girl whose beauty was incredibly strange and slightly out of place, even in a city like New York. In Josi's case, her long, stark-white hair and almost clear blue eyes were accented by two strange spots of freckles underneath her eyes. Her sharp and perfectly contoured nose had a small patch of freckles across the bridge. Razor thin and lanky, she stood at six feet, three inches tall. Her height compounded her strangeness and allure.

Over the years, she had become used to people staring at her— not necessarily because she was pulchritudinous, but because she just looked so unusual. Sometimes at Yankee Stadium, children would pull annoyingly on their parent's arm and point at her. It was as if someone had carefully peeled her off a painting and dropped her onto the sidewalks of Manhattan, like a carnival sideshow. On her almost daily trips around the city, tourists would often take photos of her, thinking she must be some type of celebrity.

She was well aware that more than one of her students and fellow teachers crushed on her—a fact that she seemed to find endlessly amusing and curiously odd. She was a good teacher, and both her students and colleagues liked her well enough to make her day-by-day teaching life mostly pleasurable. She would never be named best teacher in New York, but she certainly could have a nice career if she continued on the education path.

She had always been a quirky girl, and as the years ticked by, Josi began to feel as if her senses were becoming tuned in a way she really didn't understand. At times, she found herself in a semi-hypnotic state, with visions of color and images swiping across her inner eyes. Often, she found herself frozen in the shower or on the train, unable to move while strange pops of light and fire filled her head. Strangely, it was not at all unpleasant or concerning to her, and deep down she knew they must mean *something*, but her mind's eye was just not able to put the pieces together. Not yet, anyway.

Despite the incredibly strange and bizarrely eccentric skin she had grown up in, her childhood in Hell's Kitchen was normal and full of pleasant memories. She was adopted by a nice but considerably older couple when she was an infant. Her adoptive father was a captain in the New York City Fire Department, and her adoptive mother was a seamstress in the Garment District.

The orphanage closed shortly after Josi was adopted, and no records were ever found on where Josi came from or how she came to reside at the orphanage. Sister Mary Margaret first took Josi to meet her adoptive parents when she was just an infant. Mr. and Mrs. Andolini fell instantly in love. When Sister Mary Margaret and a counselor from child services first opened the bassinet to introduce the Andolinis to their new daughter, they were awestruck and speechless. Never had they seen a child with clear blue eyes and bone-white hair, accented by spots of freckles under her eyes and across her nose. Even at that tender age, it was clear she was going to be a tall and striking girl. Marylin Andolini looked at her new daughter and whispered, "My God."

She looked wide-eyed at her husband, Pete, and then at the caseworker, who was grinning.

"I have never seen a child with such distinct and strange beauty. She is honestly breathtaking," the caseworker said and squeezed Josi's tiny fingers.

Sister Mary Margaret and the caseworker sat down at the kitchen table with what little paperwork they had on Josi. She had no birth certificate and no medical records. The state doctor had examined her just days before and determined her to be in perfect health, but the caseworker recommended they take Josi to their family physician as soon as possible. Mr. and Mrs. Andolini both agreed and would make an appointment right away.

Sister Mary Margaret never did tell the Andolinis how she received a strange phone call late one evening from a woman who simply identified herself as Amanda Kendall. She asked that Sister Mary Margaret come to one of the large buildings in midtown Manhattan the following morning to see her about a child who needed to be placed in a caring home as soon as possible.

The following morning, Sister Mary Margaret took the train to the monstrous glass building and rode the elevator to the twenty-third floor. As the elevator doors swished open, she was immediately welcomed, rather coldly, by Amanda Kendall and two men in black suits. They all wore badges that said *FBI* in big, blue letters. They took her through an office full of men and women who barely spoke and didn't look up from their computer screens as she walked through. Sister Mary Margaret found it odd that no one took notice of a nun walking through the catacombs of their office.

They stepped into a typical-looking conference room with a large, round table in the center. Several plants adorned the corners, and there was a green chalkboard on the wall. A large American flag hung in the far corner. In the center of the table were a single manila envelope, a pitcher of water, and a small stack of plastic cups. Sister Mary Margaret noticed the room smelled like new carpeting and paint.

The two men in black suits waited outside the conference room while Amanda Kendall closed the door. Sister Mary Margaret may have been a simple nun, but she was a clever and observant one. Being in charge of orphaned children for so many years had sharpened her senses and power of observation greatly. As soon as she was seated, she quickly glanced at the lone file on the table. Miss Kendall quickly, and almost nonchalantly, scooped up the folder to keep the cover hidden. Too late. Sister Mary Margaret saw the single, mechanically written line. It simply read: *Above Top Secret—Star Child. SETI/NORAD Eyes Only.*

Later that night, Amanda Kendall and the two men in black suits pulled up to the orphanage in a plain blue sedan with government license plates. Sister Mary Margaret was waiting for them at the curb. They handed her the bassinet and left almost immediately. She never saw or heard from them again.

The Andolinis lived on Forty-Seventh Street in a large apartment on the top floor. As a kid, Josi would sneak onto the roof of their pre-war building and gaze upward into the vastness of space.

Her father would ask her, "Josi-Bear, what are you doing up on that ol' roof, anyway?"

"I don't know, Daddy. Sometimes the stars ... sometimes they twinkle extra bright, like they want to tell me something," little Josi would sheepishly reply and look down at her feet.

Her daddy would tease her; he would smack her on the butt with the rolled-up newspaper and bark, "Do they tell you to go get washed up for supper?" Josi would squeal with laughter and run into the bathroom to wash her hands.

The week Josi started college, both of her parents were tragically killed in an auto accident. Her dad had run a red light, and they were broadsided by a car driven by two middle-aged women on their way to church in Queens. By the grace of God, both the women walked away, but Josi's parents were killed instantly.

She blamed herself for the accident, as she knew damn well her father was getting too old to be driving. She kept putting off the awkward conversation she knew she needed to have with him about selling the old Buick and getting him subway and bus passes.

During the years that followed her parents' deaths, she was generally on a form of soft autopilot. School, home, Yankees games, repeat. She lived her life and enjoyed her baseball games, her Netflix, and her growing collection of secondhand books about baseball.

That all seemed to change one summer night when Josi was in her little kitchen, washing and drying a single plate, fork, spoon, knife, and glass. The windows were open, and the city sounds of sirens and car horns floated through the apartment like familiar and expected ghosts.

She was leaning against the sink listening to her Yankees beat up on the Red Sox at Fenway Park when her legs suddenly started to shake uncontrollably. All of a sudden, the Yankees were a million miles away, and her head started to buzz and tickle. She heard a voice in her head calling her name, ever so softly.

Josi ... Josi ... it's Colly.

She squeezed her eyes tight and tried to focus on whatever was invading her mind.

In an instant, she dropped the plate she was drying and bolted through the apartment. With her long legs, she jumped over the couch in a single, leaping bound to the window, where she stuck her head out into the night. Her white hair blew around in circles, just as a fire truck sped by, lights and sirens blazing.

Her pale-blue eyes scanned back and forth, up and down, and finally focused on a dot of light deep in the night sky. It was a very specific dot this time—not just a cluster of stars, but a very specific star. She stayed locked and focused on the star for a long minute, then slowly pulled herself back into the apartment. The voice was gone, her legs quit shaking, and the Yankees were still beating up on the Red Sox.

She took one step away from the window and stopped. Her mouth fell open and her blue eyes sparkled. She drew in a deep breath that exacerbated the puzzled look on her face. Something, or someone, was coming.

Colly. Permission Slip.
Soon-to-be Outlaw

COLLY STOOD WITH HER ARMS CROSSED ON her huge marble balcony, which overlooked one of the three massive seas of tranquility on the northernmost tip of the planet Gliese. The six great moons of Gliese hung in a sort of semicircle across the early-evening sky, while a constant and stunningly beautiful shower of meteors crisscrossed the sky in random patterns and colors.

Her long, jet-black hair blew in twists and curls as the warm solar breeze wrapped itself around her. Her strangely tall and lanky body twisted as she turned to face away from the setting sun and looked into the dark side of the Gliesen sky.

Childlike, she counted the shooting stars that consistently tracked across the deep black and pink sky.

"One star, two star, three star, four," she whispered to herself.

Her pale-blue, almost clear eyes scanned the skies until she found what she was looking for: a distant and faint star that she knew well. The star of Calamaroon. Three planets out from the center was Earth. Three planets out was her Gemini sister.

Ever since Colly was a small child, she knew—or perhaps *felt* her twin. An ancient longing felt almost constantly for a twin she had never seen, except in her dreams and visions.

She knew her twin was an orphan, like she was. An orphan stranded on the primitive planet Earth. She knew her twin had gifts that would be wildly unusual on Earth, *if* she was able to channel them. She knew she was kind, smart, and attentive. Most of all, she knew she needed to find her. It was as if something in the center of her brain ached and itched; something in her *soul* ached.

Earlier that day, she had stood in front of the Council of Generalship and again pleaded her case to the nine-person panel of senators. She had stood in front of the nine counselors before. As a matter of fact, this was the third time she had appeared in front of the prestigious board. The first two hearings had not gone well for Colly. Both of the previous times, she was denied permission to travel to Earth and find her sister. The council allowed for only two appeals, and after that, they would no longer hear her case.

She calmly walked up to the podium and slightly rolled her shoulders back. The massive room was empty except for Colly, the council, and a few other people with the Hall of Records who had the job of recording the proceedings between Colly and the council.

She again asked for permission to travel to Earth. She presented her case in great detail and with sincerity. Colly was asking the council for permission to travel to Earth to find and bring home her Gemini, a Star Child and her twin, who was living as an earthling and had been doing so for twenty-two Earth years.

Not even the council could reveal what led to her Gemini being lost in the Milky Way Galaxy. The circumstances on how she, Colly, was able to return to Gliese and her twin was not eluded her all her life. All the public records showed, and all Colly could ever discover, was that her mother was a Star Traveler who was killed close to the Calamaroon Star. All other details had been wiped clear, and the council refused to elaborate or break their silence on the circumstances.

On her many trips to the Hall of Records, Colly was able to find only one reference to her mother. She was a Star Traveler and a great warrior. Her name was Calista, but no other information about her existed. She was able to locate a single, grainy photograph of her sitting on the fuselage of an orb. Colly smiled and teared up—she looked like her mother.

"You have no idea if your Gemini is alive or even exists. That being said, for the sake of argument, let's say your instincts are correct and you do have a Gemini alive on Earth. You can't tell us where she resides on Earth, what she does, or even if she wants to leave her earthly life to return to Gliese. We cannot allow you to embark on a cosmic fishing expedition on the belief that your feelings and instincts are 100 percent accurate," the grand counselor, Pancros, said.

"They are accurate, and of course she wants to come home! She is not an earthling; she is Gliese!" Colly's blue eyes filled with tears as she pleaded. She was becoming desperate and exasperated.

"We have been through this many times, Colly," the counselor continued, ignoring Colly's logic and growing slightly impatient. "The rule of law is very clear. You are not permitted to leave the Centurion Belt under any circumstances. The risk to your life and of showing our presence to others is too risky."

"She is alive! I can feel her, Counselors. I can find her. I need to find her. I am asking for your blessing, your help, and your permission. Please!"

The emotionless council sat stone-faced.

"The council has spoken. We must deny you."

Colly stood on the balcony for a long time staring up at the star Calamaroon. From time to time, her attention would be diverted elsewhere in the sky, but she would always return her gaze to that one star. Her entire life had been spent looking at the heavens and looking toward the east, toward Calamaroon.

As a child growing up in a home for abandoned children, Colly would sneak out of her tiny room, clad only in a pair of long, white pajamas, and carefully make her way out to the large, open courtyard that bordered the old, seven-story building. She would stand there looking up to the heavens, holding her little stuffed toy in her hand. She would drop her head straight back and gently blow her sweet, innocent breath straight into the night sky.

Kissy for my sissy, she would whisper in her head to her sister, who was some twenty light-years away from her. Even at that young age, she knew her sister could hear her. She knew she could hear her whispers dance across the heavens and find her on Earth.

On one cool spring night, Colly stood out in the courtyard looking up to the heavens, and one of the teachers walked quickly out into the night.

"Colly! What are you doing out here?" she asked exasperatedly and looked around.

"I'm talking to my sister," Colly said sheepishly.

"Your sister? Colly, sweetheart, you don't have a sister," the teacher said quietly, confused.

"I do have a sister," Colly said matter-of-factly.

Colly gently looked upward and smiled. The solar breeze blew her hair around in small circles, while somewhere in the distance the sound of the tram roared by, echoing through the courtyard.

"Your sister—is she in heaven, honey?" the teacher asked gently.

Colly smiled and slowly pointed straight up into the Gliesen night sky. She shook her head and bit her lip. "She's not in heaven; she's *in the heavens.*"

The teacher stared at her, wide-eyed, as the solar wind continued to gust and swirl around them.

As Colly grew older, her life generally settled into a rather successful pattern for a girl on Gliese. She was adopted at the age of fourteen by a rather eccentric couple that provided her with everything and every opportunity she would need. Her childhood, like her sister's, was happy and uncomplicated. As a teenager, she excelled in sports and school and read with a strange voracity that sometimes alarmed her parents.

By the time she turned sixteen, Colly was close to six feet tall and extraordinarily beautiful. Her classmates at school secretly stared at her in awe. She was smart, clever, and funny, while maintaining an aura of kindness. As she got older, Colly began to discover that her mind seemed to focus on things in a way that left her somewhat astonished. Sometimes, she was able to feel things, and if she focused enough, words that she was not meant to hear came to her from other people.

On her seventeenth birthday, her aunt Michelle placed a large, wrapped box on the kitchen table next to her birthday cake. Colly smiled and looked down at the box.

"Well, can you guess what it is?" her aunt said jokingly.

Colly felt numb. In that quick tick of the clock, she knew it was a new camera. She knew her aunt had bought it at a small camera store. She knew her aunt had chatted with the store owner about the upcoming elections. She knew her aunt had worn a red top and a blue skirt. She knew everything that had happened at that camera store. Then, in an instant, the vision faded, like a dream from the night before might fade as the day goes on.

"Is it a new camera?" Colly asked weakly.

Her aunt smiled hugely. "It is! Way to go, Colly!"

Colly smiled and bit her lip. Later that night, she lay in bed trying to wrap her mind around what was happening. It was as if she was going through some strange form of mental puberty. Changes to her mind were happening, and she couldn't quite figure out what they meant. She closed her eyes and found sleep. It would be several years before another incident like that one would make an appearance.

At university, she studied construction and engineering and settled into a job designing homes and large office buildings. It was a job that she found surprisingly rewarding. Like her twin, she was a loner and never married or had children. In her late teens, she started to piece together the plan to find her sister. She began studying maps of the universe and learned everything she could about wormholes and Earth culture. Of course, she was a good citizen and had faith that if she pleaded her case to council, they would grant her permission to travel to Earth and rescue her sister. Sadly, for Colly, this was not to be.

The stark realization was that she was almost out of options—almost. The council had ruled against her for the third and final time.

There was to be no appeal, no plea for mercy and justice. It was now over—or was it?

Colly turned quickly and went inside. The breeze off the sea was growing stronger, and she could feel the temperature start to rise dramatically. Clouds began to quickly black out the moons one by one. A cosmic rain was coming.

She ate a late, solitary dinner, which was her norm. In her mind's eye, she kept pondering her last option—her last chance to rescue her sister and bring her home to Gliese.

Once she had finished her dinner, she washed her single plate, fork, spoon, knife, and glass and retired to her couch, where several books on Earth's culture lay open. She continued her reading on Earth and its people, but she quickly realized she was having a hard time focusing on her books tonight. With a deep breath, she closed her book and went to the bathroom. As she brushed her teeth, she took a long look at herself in the mirror. Was her sister like her? Did she have the same pale, clear-blue eyes? What about the freckles that accented her eyes and nose? Was her hair this deep black too? Was she also tall?

Someday—someday soon, she would know.

She lay in her bed that night, and the rain did indeed come. Sheets of warm rainwater lashed against her windows relentlessly. The rolling thunder was constant. Colly lay back and cried. Her eyes were wide open, catching the reflection of the lightning in her large, mysterious pupils.

She tried to set her moral compass to neutral. She had to break the law to get to Earth,; that was now clear. This was something she had never done. If she was caught, and the odds weare she would be, wais it worth it? Yes. What if she was unable to find her Gemini? What if Earth was a hostile, lawless place, like some say it issaid it was? She took a deep, shaky breath and flipped her pillow over to the cool side. The last trick the universe had up its sleeve was the most frightening. What if she got stranded on Earth?

Despite her fears and reservations, her last option was now her only option: a. A smuggler. A pirate of sorts. She needed an orb to travel in. The cCouncil would not provide her with an intergalactic orb, but a pirate would. Oh, my yes, ... a pirate wouldill.

It was, of course, risky and against the law, for starters. Most disturbing was the risk to her and her sister. Colly was well aware that the odds of the return orb being able to land exactly where it should be was only about 5 percent. That meant that there was an overwhelming chance Colly could never come back to Gliese and she would be marooned on Earth like her sister.

She began to sob as she ran the statistics through her head. *Five percent. Five percent.* The number swirled in her head like some strange ballet dancer. She took a long mental look at the life she had here on Gliese. Of course, she had her work and a small circle of friends, but no real blood family. This constant ache was slowly wearing her down. It was like an itch that desperately needed scratching, perhaps at any cost.

There were many details to work out. Leaving Gliese without getting detected, mapping the wormholes and black holes, figuring out where her Gemini was living on Earth, and learning enough Earth culture to blend in. It was daunting on the surface and she was sure with every layer she peeled off, another obstacle would be there to deal with. It would drain her mentally and physically, but love will find a way. She would find a way to Earth. Oh yes, she would find a way.

3

Bad Bobby Underwood. Locker Room Fun. X-Rated

BAD BOBBY UNDERWOOD LIT A CIGARETTE AND waved out the match with a quick flick of his wrist. From his small third-floor apartment on Eighth Avenue in Manhattan, he had a clear view of the street and sidewalk below. He leaned against the window frame and watched the people hurry by, looking at them as if they were strange bugs.

He smiled slyly and thought to himself, *Fuckin' cunts.*

Bad Bobby took a long drag from his Winston and held the smoke. His disdain for the general public, especially women, was palpable, to say the least. He radiated contempt for just about everything and everyone who crossed his path.

His apartment was in a perpetual state of darkness and cluttered with stacks of books and magazines tossed haphazardly everywhere. The vast majority of them dealt with UFOs and paranormal subjects. Sprinkled throughout were magazines about torture and the Third Reich, underground magazines about animal killings, pornography, and other assorted debauchery. The carpet was burnt orange and mangy. On the wall closest to the front door, which was adorned with multiple locks, was a huge poster of an alien from a pulp-fiction novel with the caption: "See you soon, motherfucker!"

Two huge metal desks took up most of the apartment, along with a beat-up couch and an old, outdated television. Pizza boxes, beer cans, and a multitude of overflowing ashtrays dotted the living room's landscape. The apartment smelled like corn chips, dirty socks, and trapped cigarette smoke.

The kitchen, bath, and single bedroom were in the same filthy and cluttered condition. Not even Bobby remembered the last time his sheets on the single bed were changed. The top drawer of the old 1970s nightstand next to the bed held a 1918 German Luger gun with three bullets in the clip, which he had stolen from his grandfather.

The second drawer down contained several bras and panties: six pairs of panties and five bras, to be exact. Most of the panties were ripped. Toward the back were several pieces of women's jewelry, including a high school ring with a pink stone. Engraved on the side of the ring was the name *Patricia*.

Almost daily, Bobby would open the drawer and rifle through its contents. Every time he did so, he would scold himself for not getting rid of the items. Even Bobby realized that it was incredibly foolish to save such trophies, no matter how much sexual gratification they gave him.

The metal desks in the living room were crammed with shortwave radios, police scanners, and a hodgepodge of electronic devices. They constantly buzzed with police, fire, and military personnel chatter. A thick, black wire ran out the window to the roof, where Bobby had clandestinely installed such a large antenna that most of the tenants just figured it to be part of the building.

Bobby had all the underground frequencies that were reserved exclusively for the use of police and other government radios and the authorized people who used them. He had hacked into many of the top-secret frequencies, which, of course, was a big, big no-no. Not that he gave a shit; it just never crossed his mind that what he hacked could land him in hot water.

He had discovered his strange curiosity of extraterrestrial life and all things odd and curious as a teenager. He had read Orson Wells' *War of the Worlds* when he was sixteen, and from that point on, his fascination with the possibility of life on other planets began to grow at an alarming rate. He became obsessed and driven to explore and discover all he could about the subject.

Every night as a teenager, he would venture into the courtyard of his parents' apartment building on Norfolk Street on the lower east side of Manhattan. He would cup his hands, light up a Winston that he stole from his old man's nightstand, and gaze upward. With every glance skyward, his mind would drift in anticipation of the day when, like in the campy sci-fi movies, the aliens would make their presence known by landing on the front lawn of the White House.

Even as a kid, he was strange and an outsider. His greasy black hair and bad acne often made him an easy target for bullies. His strangeness and oftentimes downright bizarre behavior caused his parents and teachers some concern. In the vastness of the New York school system, he was easily lost in the shuffle of the thousands upon thousands of other kids, and Bobby was never given the help he may have needed.

Bobby Underwood was a fairly nondescript thirty-year-old man. Although the word *creepy* often crossed people's quick thoughts when they made eye contact with him in the streets, they quickly forgot about him seconds later. He tended to lurch as he walked, and in his strangely narcissistic mind, that set him above the others. He was Bobby Underwood. *The* Bobby Underwood.

Around his sixteenth birthday, one of the basketball players gave Bobby the moniker of *Bad Bobby*. Between sixth and seventh period, Bobby knew if he rushed out of his World History class, he could sneak out to the back courtyard and down the alley that connected the cafeteria and kitchen to the gym. Behind a seldom-used gym door was a vent that led to the girls' locker room. If Bobby flipped one of the many milk crates stacked by the cafeteria door and stood on his tippy-toes, he had a clear view into the girls' locker room.

One day, Bobby stood on a milk crate watching the girls change, with one hand down his pants. As fate would have it, Chad Garland, star basketball player, and Ginger Orwell, head cheerleader, happened to walk by on their way to the library and see him.

"Ewwwwww ... his hand is down his pants! He's rubbing his little cock!" Ginger said loudly in disgust and covered her mouth.

Bobby immediately jumped down and ran toward the kitchen. He had one hand over his crotch to try to cover his erection.

Chad laughed and called after him. "Baaaad Bobby Underwood! Stay away from the chicks, Bad Bobby! Hey, everybody! It's Bad Bobby!" And the name stuck.

Even before the locker-room incident, he'd had very few friends, and he had even fewer as an adult. Most of his social contact was at his job in a warehouse on Fifteenth Street, where he sorted boxes of staple food goods that were sent out to restaurants and institutions throughout the tristate area. Even there, his coworkers generally stayed clear of Bad Bobby.

Of course, in the world of cyberspace and ham radio clicks, Bobby did just fine. Most of his friends were spread out all over the world, and they all seemed to share the same distrust of the government, and most of them, like Bobby, were loners. They had no idea about Bobby's secret life outside the cryptic norm of dark cyberspace. He communicated with them daily, sharing conspiracy stories and fantastic tales of half-truth encounters of aliens and government spies.

As the years ticked slowly by, Bobby stayed on that same plane of semi-weird normalcy. Only during the past five years had he become a hard-core deviant and criminal. It was as if a part of his brain was turning into mush a little more each day. His mind cultivated scenarios that he fantasized about—not just bizarre sexual fantasies and torture fetishes, but more worldly ideas.

He became convinced that there were aliens among us. When he ventured out into the city, he constantly shifted his eyes back and forth as he walked through Manhattan, looking for anything that might be a clue of another life force. Never mind that most of the indicators he looked for were from pulp-fiction novels and magazines and not based on any fact or science.

Bobby crushed out his cigarette in an overflowing ashtray next to the window and pulled open a bent and warped drawer from the stand next to the couch.

"There you are," he whispered to himself as he pulled out a soiled DVD. His erection grew as he looked at the cover, which showed two beautiful girls wrapped up in each other, holding each other's breasts.

He opened his beat-up DVD player and quickly shoved the disc in. He sat back on his couch and started to masturbate while watching the two beautiful girls perform oral sex on each other. His orgasm was bitter, quick, and angry. It was an apt reflection on how Bad Bobby Underwood lived his life.

4

Drinks with Friends. The Dream. The Zon

THE BELL RANG AT PS 51 AND A RUSH OF children noisily flooded the hallways. Josi stood by her classroom door, said goodbye to her kids, and answered quick questions as the children pushed each other out into the hall. Her eighth-grade honors English class was the last of the day and was the brightest. Her students were well behaved and as hungry for knowledge as any group of fourteen-year-olds could be at that stage in their life. As the last kid made his way out, Josi walked to the blackboard and started to erase the period's lesson with big, sweeping arches with the blackboard eraser.

"Knock, knock!" A small, pretty, red-haired woman peeked her head in the door and smiled.

"Well, hello, Grace," Josi said smoothly and smiled at the woman.

"Hiiiii … sooo," Grace chimed as she walked in slowly, "a few of us are going to Mandell's for drinks; you in?" She looked over her shoulder to make sure no children in the hall had been able to hear her.

Josi shrugged and leaned against her desk. "I have to be home by 7:05 for first pitch. Yankees and Pittsburgh Pirates tonight," she said with a grin and crossed her arms.

Grace shook her head, amused. "Seriously, Josi? First pitch? Really?"

What Grace didn't know is that Josi had absolutely no interest in going to have drinks with a group of people she barely knew outside of work and who, to be perfectly frank, she didn't care for all that much when she saw them at work. Josi sighed and reluctantly decided to give in. She was well aware that if she refused, Grace would hound her endlessly. In the end, it was just simpler to go, mask her annoyance with her coworkers, and leave.

"Fine. What time?" she asked.

Grace beamed. "Okay. See you there in like an hour? Maybe less?"

Josi nodded and smiled, and Grace turned and walked quickly out the door, as if she wanted to leave before Josi could change her mind.

Her colleagues were somewhat surprised when she walked into Mandell's Bar & Grill an hour later. None of the eight teachers and administrators sitting around the corner of the bar had actually expected her to show up. The bar was crowded with a lot of people in suits chatting about whatever it is people chat about. A great many of the men, and a few of the women, directly or indirectly watched as the lanky and striking Josi made her way to the back corner of the bar to join her fellow teachers.

"Josi!" Grace said loudly and got up off her barstool. She fell toward Josi and hugged her tightly. Josi was slightly taken aback by this strange flash of affection from her coworker. Then the scotch fumes hit her and she smiled, now understanding the hug.

For the next couple hours, Josi nursed club sodas with lime while she listened to her fellow teachers complain and snark about everything imaginable. It was strange that even though Josi said very little and stood toward the back of the group, everyone always seemed to be staring at her. Whenever someone made a comment or started a fresh conversation, they seemed to look to Josi for some kind of unspoken approval.

She watched with a twinge of contempt as her coworkers went from tipsy, to buzzed, to drunk. Because she was so much taller than her fellow teachers, she physically looked down at them as they got more out of control. She thought to herself that this was a terrific metaphor.

As six p.m. came, Josi went. She said polite goodbyes and told everyone she would see them Monday, and she headed out. It was only six blocks to her apartment, and the early spring air was refreshing and added a little bounce to her step.

Once home, Josi changed into her favorite Yankees jersey and ordered a mushroom and green-pepper pizza for dinner. She watched the game and scarfed pizza while keeping score of the game on an old notebook that held a small sleeve full of scorecards. Next to her was a bottle of her favorite soda, Grape Crush. She felt a slight twinge of nostalgia as she drank the soda. It reminded her of her father and all the afternoons they spent watching baseball games and cheering on their Yankees. Josi smiled as she circled the final score on the card: Yankees 3, Pirates 1.

An hour later, she lay in bed, and the ambient light of New York City splashed strange shadows across the bedroom walls. The low wail of sirens and car horns constantly echoed through the canyons of buildings and eventually found their way into her bedroom. Josi didn't notice the noise. As for most native New Yorkers, it was just a part of background life. It was something you never noticed until you left and realized how quiet the world outside New York really was.

She was unable to sleep, despite the late hour—well, late for Josi. She looked at the clock: 11:12 p.m. She tossed and turned and kept flipping her pillow, looking for the cool side. Once light sleep seemed to finally latch on, she found herself dreaming. In her dream, she was being pulled gently by the arm. It wasn't an unpleasant sensation, and it didn't alarm her at all. It felt almost playful, like she was a child again playing games on the street in Hell's Kitchen. She slipped deeper into sleep, and a voice called to her boldly.

Josi!

In her dream, she was a ten-year-old girl again, with skinned knees and a Yankees ball cap turned backward. She looked around, smiled, and laughed.

Everything seemed to be in muted color. Again, the soft voice called out.

Josi!

In her dream, she saw another little girl sitting on the stoop of her building in pink overalls and high-top Converse sneakers. This girl had long hair just like hers, only it was jet black. Josi ran to the girl and smiled. As she approached the girl on the stoop, she continued smiling. The little girl with the black hair looked up and grinned.

"Hi, I'm Colly," she said.

"I'm Josi," she replied as she stepped closer and bounced on her tippy-toes.

Little Colly stood up, and the girls hugged for a long time. No one on the street seemed to notice them. The fire hydrant continued to spray water, and the children's laughter floated up and down the block. There was an ice cream truck on the corner with a line of kids, and the sound of a stickball game could be heard.

Colly and Josi started to walk down the shaded, tree-lined sidewalk, holding hands. They looked like yin and yang twins, Josi with her white hair and Colly with her black. The world around them kept moving as two boys rode by on their Schwinns, laughing, off to find an adventure.

"Josi," Colly said and squeezed her hand. "I need to talk to you."

"I know," Josi said, as she squeezed back and nodded.

"I'm going to be coming here soon to get you. Is that okay? Josi, is that okay?"

"It is, but I'm afraid!" Josi said and looked at her.

Colly raised her little eyebrows and said, surprised, "Don't be afraid. Don't you ever be afraid."

Josi nodded.

The girls stopped mid-step on the sidewalk and Josi pointed down at the hopscotch squares boldly drawn in white chalk. Giggling, Colly went through the squares, bouncing from foot to foot with her arms stretched out for balance. Her black hair bounced with every step. She made it through and turned around.

"You go," she said, laughing.

Josi followed suit and the pair started walking again, giggling.

Colly held open her hand and there was a piece of fat chalk in her palm. Josi looked at the chalk as they walked along and then she looked up at Colly, confused.

"Josi, listen to me," Colly said. "Find a piece of chalk like this, and we'll write a little code around the city. Let's write 'C&J' on walls. That means we know we know we are getting close. Don't write anything else, because people will be looking for us and we can't give them any clues. Just write our code and focus on me, and I'll focus on you."

Josi beamed and said, "That's a really great idea, Colly! Especially since when I grow up, I'm going to be a teacher, and I'll have plenty of chalk."

The pair walked in silence for a moment.

"We look exactly alike," Josi said and looked at Colly as they walked slowly down the sidewalk.

"You're my Gemini, silly," Colly replied.

The resemblance was amazingly and hauntingly perfect, right down to the exact freckle pattern that highlighted the space under their eyes. Their eyes were the same: pale but deep at the same time. If you were able to get nose to nose and look deep into them, you might notice the color swirling. It looked as if a tiny galaxy was in constant, slow rotation.

"I have something for you," Colly said with a smile. They stopped and Colly held out her hand again. In her palm was an incredibly beautiful, round gem. It was about the size of a pinball, and it glowed a deep and vibrant blue.

"Is that for me?" Josi asked, wide-eyed.

"It's called a Zon," Colly said and smiled.

Very carefully, Josi took the Zon and looked deeply at the unearthly gem.

"It's so pretty," she said and Colly smiled, pleased that Josi liked it.

Josi put the Zon in her front pocket and hugged Colly. They held hands and began walking and talking again. At the end of the block, Josi stopped abruptly and tugged at Colly's hand.

"I'm not allowed any farther than this. Daddy said so."

"It's going to be okay, Josi," Colly said and squeezed her hand again before she let go. She continued talking as she started walking across the street.

"I'll see you soon. I promise. Let's find each other, Josi! Look for me, Josi! Focus on me! Breathe deep and you'll feel me!"

In an instant, the sun started to fade. A deep fog began to cover the street, and Colly started to drift away.

"Josi, Josi! Focus, Josi! Find me, Gemini!" Colly yelled as the fog slowly engulfed her and she started to fade from sight.

"Colly! Colly! Colly!" Josi screamed for her sister.

Bright light filled Josi's world, and she covered her face and looked down. Colly was gone.

When morning came, Josi sat up in bed and rubbed her eyes. She had to pee badly. The dream was still incredibly fresh in her head, and her body had an odd tingle to it. Her mouth tasted like she had been sucking on a penny. She rubbed her face with her hands and closed her eyes. She felt slightly perplexed and strangely excited.

With a deep sigh, she threw her legs off the bed and stood up. She looked down between her feet as she heard a light thump on the flooring and the sound of something rolling across her hardwood floors. It was a brilliant-blue Zon. The same Zon Colly had given her in the dream. Josi forgot she needed to go to the bathroom.

"Oh. My. Fuck," Josi said softly as the Zon rolled slowly across the floor and stopped when it bumped into one of her Converse sneakers.

·

5

Big Plans. Fietch the Space Pirate. Space Girl Colly

OPEN BOOKS AND PAPERS COVERED THE table in the living room as night closed in on Gliese. A small stack of handwritten notes sat off to the side; several had fallen off the table and landed on the floor. Written on the papers in Colly's handwriting were scribbles on how to drive a car, information on Earth money, and slang. A picture of Elvis Presley lay next to them. Her laptop computer was open to a page with the title "Earth Music and Dance."

Colly was asleep on the couch next to the table, wearing a pair of sweats and an oversized, floppy T-shirt with a picture of a huge ice cream cone on it. She woke suddenly and stared at the ceiling. Her heart was beating loudly in her chest, and she seemed to be having a hard time catching her breath. Finally, with a deep inhale, she sat up and looked at the table with all the earthly materials on it and smiled. She had just seen her sister for the first time and felt a little disconcerted and giddy.

Two days earlier, Colly ramped up her mission to learn as much as she could about modern Earth culture. She found it both maddening and amusing at the same time. Finding the information was easy, as many books and study programs existed to teach anyone about Earth basics. She already knew a great deal about Earth, having taken several classes during her time at university, and with a plethora of information at her fingertips, she felt more than ready.

On the morning of her impromptu advanced Earth education, she woke early and caught the tram to the outer marks of the city. It was a dangerous and dirty place, to be sure, but Colly was a warrior like her mother and her sister and would show no fear.

She kept her eyes closed as the tram launched itself across the Gliesen landscape at blistering speeds. Her temples ached from the mental voyage she had taken to visit Josi and let her know she was coming. One thing she now knew for sure was that Josi was alive and living in New York City, which was one of the planet's largest metropolises. Once she got to Earth, she would have to count on Josi looking for her as much as she was looking for Josi.

She stepped off the tram and walked the six dirty blocks to a rather nondescript block building whose weathered and faded facade read: "Yellowjackets Bar. Fine Food and Drink!" The neighboring buildings were mostly dilapidated, and many were vacant. The building and the sign above the door were just as they were described by an underworld friend Colly knew through a job she once had at a betting parlor in the city of Lincs while she was in school.

When she was denied passage by council, she contacted her acquaintance and asked him if he could possibly facilitate a meeting between her and the type of person who may be able to help. He gave Colly the name and address of a smuggler that could help her get to Earth—for a price, of course.

Colly pulled on the front door, which was locked. She peered in the dusty window and didn't see any movement. After a brief moment of thought, she walked through the tight alley around back. The smell of garbage, urine, and oil hung in the air.

Behind the bar was a large, open-area courtyard with a leaning garage full of discarded orb parts, scrap space debris, and what Colly could only assume were lines of stolen aero cars. Several men were standing around, talking in low voices. As soon as Colly turned the corner, the dangerous-looking men turned and glared at her. One man smiled slyly and looked her up and down, stopping at her crotch. Colly didn't bat an eye. She stepped forward in defiance and stared down the men, almost challenging them to a confrontation. She cut an imposing figure with her height and build like that of an exotic cat.

"Which one of you is Fietch?" Colly asked with authority.

To her left, a small, pudgy man stepped out of the shadows and wiped his hands with a dirty rag.

"Who's asking?" he asked.

Colly turned to the dirty little man and asked, with a hint of surprise and amusement, "You're Fietch?"

The man opened his arms and smiled.

"I am Fietch." He started to chuckle, as did Colly.

"My name is Colly."

"So, how can I help you, Colly?" Fietch asked as they sat in the dark and dirty bar surrounded by a sea of barstools that were flipped onto tables. A neon sign buzzed and flickered behind the bar, and the place smelled like alcohol and cigarettes. Colly looked around the dark bar and noticed a man leaning in the doorway. She looked at Fietch and nodded in the direction of the shadowy figure.

"Books!" Fietch said, looking at the man. "Take a walk!" The shadowy figure scowled, turned, and walked out.

Colly smiled, and she and Fietch stared at each other. Finally, Colly exhaled and spoke.

"We have a mutual friend who suggested I speak with you about…" Colly paused, looked around, and continued, "… getting me to the Calamaroon star. More specifically, Earth."

"Earth!" Fietch said, coughing and laughing. His smoker's cough lingered, and he spat into a handkerchief. "Why in the holy shit do you want to go to Earth? Have they discovered fire yet?" He smirked while leaning back in his chair.

Colly leaned back in her chair, mimicked Fietch, and crossed her arms.

"My sister is there. I want to go get her and bring her home. Not that it's any of your concern."

"Well," Fietch said and smiled, "everything is my concern. And it's not cheap, and it's risky for both of us, especially you. First, you need to map the wormholes, then figure out how to avoid Gliese security tracking you, and then you have—"

Colly leaned forward and held up her slender hand.

"I know the risks, thank you."

"Do you?" he asked solemnly.

"Do you know that without a manned craft, the odds of the remote pickup being there are less than 5 percent? Do you know you probably will be stuck there forever? That is, unless you can find someone stupid enough to pilot a craft to Earth to pick you up." Fietch bellowed with laughter.

"I know what I'm getting into," she said and looked around the dark bar.

"Well then, you must know the more risk *I* take, the more money it costs *you*. You'll need a reliable orb, with a return remote orb, bribes for the patrols in the outer layers … all this can be traced back to *me*."

"I have plenty of money. Do you have a reliable orb that can make the trip?" she asked.

"Oh, I have an orb, yes … but it doesn't have a cloak, so even the most primitive tracking, like Earth's, will see you coming a million miles away. They will track you as soon as your ass leaves the folds of space."

"You let me worry about that," she said, staring at him.

"When are you going?" he asked.

Colly's eyes squinted ever so slightly at the question. "Soon, tonight. I feel like I know enough about Earth culture to get by well enough to blend in. Their history and customs are rich and complicated, but I'll be just fine."

Fietch grunted and laughed. "What's to know? They are a primitive people who probably will be extinct in a thousand years."

Colly looked at him. "Not from what I've read," she said matter-of-factly. "They are a clever species of people who you are underestimating greatly."

"They did gives themselves roll and rock and Buddy Presley," Fietch said.

Colly dismissed the Earth pop-culture error and stood up. She reached in her back pocket, pulled out a wad of cash, and tossed it on the table with a little thump. Fietch raised his eyebrows in creepy approval.

"That's half," Colly said and leaned in toward him. "The rest, when I leave. Is that a deal?"

"Sure. As long as I am paid in full when you leave, little girl. The odds of you making it home are almost zero, so I want my money, Space Girl. It's a deal," Fietch said as he counted the money quickly and nodded.

Colly stood up and started for the door. "I'll be back later today. Make sure everything is ready, especially the orb."

Fietch smiled and grunted. "Okay, Space Girl. You go find your sister, and try not to get killed—or worse, stranded along the way!"

The pudgy space pirate started to laugh a dirty and disgusting laugh that made Colly cringe.

"Oh! By the way," Colly said as she started out the door. "It's *rock and roll*, not roll and rock and it's *Buddy Holly*, not Buddy Presley."

Colly smiled and slammed the door before he could reply. She muttered under her breath, "Moron."

6

Frankenberry. Mrs. Cocca. Go Yanks!

BACK ON EARTH, JOSI SAT ON HER WINDOW ledge eating an oversized bowl of Frankenberry cereal for breakfast. Her white hair was pulled up in a messy bun, and she still had on her oversized Rolling Stones T-shirt. The Stones shirt was her father's, one of the few things that she kept when her parents died. Her aunt Martina, her mom's sister, had taken care of the affairs involving the apartment and personal items. Josi asked for very little. She did ask for the Stones T-shirt and a few other odds and ends, which her aunt gladly gave to her. Josi was also the lone recipient of the life insurance policy. This enabled her to buy her own apartment and have a very nice nest egg.

Spending money and saving it was never a problem with Josi Andolini. Aside from daily expenditures like utilities and groceries, Josi only spent fun money on her Yankees tickets, her baseball book collection, and her boyish hobby of baseball-card collecting. Once or twice a season, Josi would splurge big and get herself a ticket behind home plate or behind one of the dugouts. On one occasion, Josi bought a ticket behind the visitors' dugout, and the first baseman from the Florida Marlins, Logan Morrison, winked at her and tossed her a baseball. That night when she got home, she placed it on the shelf that held all her baseball cards and books.

She scanned the street below, watching the people walk by on their way to destinations unknown. As she scooped the pink cereal into her mouth, she looked up at the Empire State Building. One of the great things about her little apartment was the perfect view of the iconic building. Sometimes when she looked out at the skyscraper, she would imagine King Kong shimmying up from floor to floor and smile to herself.

From across Forty-Fourth Street, Mrs. Cocca, Josi's favorite neighbor, stuck her head out the window, smiled, and waved at her.

"Did you see the game last night, Josi-girl?" she yelled from across the street in her thick Italian accent.

"Sure did! Go Yankees!" Josi yelled back.

"We gonna go to a game soon, right? Like we did last year?" Mrs. Cocca asked Josi.

"We sure are! I can't wait!" she assured her.

After waving a quick goodbye and blowing a kiss to Mrs. Cocca, she walked into the kitchen and poured herself another heaping bowl of cereal. She leaned against the fridge as she smashed every bite and stared at the counter across from her.

Sitting on the kitchen counter on a neatly folded paper towel was the Zon, the beautiful gift from her sister, Colly. She picked it up for probably the hundredth time that morning. It was heavy and beautifully mesmerizing. Any small and lingering doubts that she had ever had about her sister and her unique situation were now washed away.

She knew now that her sister was absolutely real and that she needed to find her. New York was a huge place, but she needed to start somewhere. As improbable as it sounded, Josi felt her best bet was to just walk out her front door and start looking. She had yet to be able to get any real sense of where Colly might be other than in New York, or soon to be in New York. She had yet to get the sense that Colly was actually here, but she knew she was coming.

She washed out her bowl and laid it to dry, then jumped into the shower and got ready for her day. Just in case she was going to be gone all day, she set her DVR to record the Yankees game in Cleveland at 1:05 p.m. "Go Yanks," she mumbled under her breath as she walked out the door.

7

Bon Voyage. Earth Goggles

COLLY HAD CAREFULLY LAID OUT HER SUPPLIES on her bed the morning she went to see Fietch for the first time. She knew if she struck a deal, she was going to probably leave that evening and wanted to be packed and ready to go.

She had a few changes of clothes that she felt would closely match the style of modern-day New York. If all else failed, she could buy what she needed at one of the thousands of boutiques she had read about in New York. Her toothbrush, hair-care items, and medicine were packed in a separate little bag. She had thousands of American dollars in a neat pile, and an American Express credit card that she meticulously designed and printed. When she was constructing the account information that would easily fool the card readers, she made the card with no limit on funds.

She carefully and quickly began to neatly pack everything into her backpack. She was dressed in rather plain Earth clothes: a pair of light-blue skinny jeans and a white hoodie. She felt this was inconspicuous enough if she got into any trouble and needed to blend in. She wasn't expecting anything like that, but she was prepared.

The night before, she had cleaned her house, written letters to her friends and adoptive family, and left a list of passwords and financial information, and in a plain, white envelope, she left a note explaining in great detail where she was and what she had done and why. All this was in the event that she actually ended up getting killed on Earth, like the pirate Fietch had said. Of course, a more likely scenario would be her and Josi getting stuck on Earth. The number ran through her head again: 5 percent.

She took one last walk around her house and stepped out onto the balcony. She drew in a deep breath and closed her eyes. The afternoon star's warmth felt good on her face, and she wondered if the Earth's star, Calamaroon, was going to feel the same way. Colly took one last look at the beautiful sea and then quickly turned around and stepped inside.

Much to her surprise, she felt a slight sting of tears as she locked the big, glass balcony door. She silently prayed that the next time she stood on the balcony, her sister would be standing next to her. She smiled through the tears as she thought about the look on her sister's face when she saw the beautiful night sky of Gliese.

A short time later, the tram stopped on the platform and Colly jumped on. Nine stops ahead were Yellowjackets Bar and the orb. All she needed to do was program the navigation system and she would be off. However, according to Fietch, this could take several hours, even with a good map.

The tram ride lasted about an hour, and during the ride, she mentally rehearsed everything she had prepared for. She went through the scenario if she got caught by the authorities in New York. How she would handle a malfunction in the orb, and how she was going to find Josi. What would happen if she missed her return window? Exactly what she would do if, like the statistics said, she got stuck there. She had to confront the realization that if things didn't go exactly as planned, she would be stuck on Earth. Because she had been denied by council, no one would know where she was, so no one would be coming to rescue her. That was a scenario that she didn't want to think about for too long, so she quickly brushed it from her thoughts.

Colly turned and looked out the window of the tram as it passed through the Great Water Plains. Miles of waterfalls spilled around the mountains of ancient rock. The blue-and-green water seemed to flow both up and down. She thought to herself how wonderful it was going to be for her and Josi to come here.

Colly cringed at the thought of never seeing this again, with or without her sister. Everything had to go according to plan. It had to. Five percent.

Two hours later, Colly sat cross-legged in the orb, programming the navigation system carefully. In her hand, she held a primitive galaxy map that she got from the national library. This was not an easy task, considering the thousands of possible wormholes and black holes; it was something that needed to be done carefully or you could end up in another time, millions of light-years away. She kept checking the map, then programming the next leg of the trip.

Earth was many light-years away, but the trip itself would be almost instantaneous. She wasn't sure where she would come out above Earth. She didn't think it likely that she would come through near New York, but that, too, didn't really matter.

Out of the corner of her eye, Colly saw Fietch coming over. Frustrated, she took a deep breath and mentally prepared to deal with the dirty space pirate.

"Hi, Space Girl!" Fietch leaned into the orb and hacked, laughing and coughing simultaneously. His breath smelled of whiskey.

Colly curled her upper lip and slid as far as she could get from him. "What do you want, Fietch? I'm busy," she asked impatiently.

"I have a little something for you. A gift, if you like." He chuckled and coughed into his hand. "Do you want it?"

"Sure, Fietch. What is it?" she asked with pushed patience.

Fietch held up a pair of vintage Earth aviator goggles. He swung them back and forth in front of Colly. His grin was monstrous and his broken, dirty teeth showed.

"What the fuck are those?" Colly asked incredulously as she snapped them from his fat pygmy hand.

"They are Earth aero-plane goggles!" he roared, laughing. "They are a good luck charm!"

Colly looked at them closely and tapped the lens a few times while turning them over in her hands.

"Where did you get these?" she asked.

"Don't you worry about that, my little Space Girl! Who knows, maybe you'll need them on Earth! You certainly will need luck!" he said and waddled away.

Colly watched him for a second and shook her head. She took one last look at the goggles and tossed them nonchalantly on the floor of the orb.

"Stupid fucking Earth goggles," she muttered under her breath as she continued the laborious task of programming the orb.

An hour later, she was ready. Her pack was next to her, and the computer was programmed. Colly, Fietch, and several of his men pushed the orb out of the oily garage and onto a patch of dirt. The men stepped away and walked toward the back door of the bar.

Colly sat down in the orb and prepared the launch cycle. Fietch knelt beside the hatch, looking uncharacteristically serious and somber.

"Look ... as soon as you come out of space, be prepared to be tracked. Earth people are primitive, but they are also aggressive and dangerous. Be prepared for it." Colly nodded quickly.

"Also, remember, it's possible the return orb will be waiting. Focus on it. You'll know where it is. If it's not there when you get there, it's. Not. Coming." Fietch emphasized the last three words by tapping on her shoulder.

"You'll be on your own. As soon as you see it's not there, move on. Don't wait. It's not going to miraculously show up. Be at the pickup zone, and don't be days late. If by some miracle the orb makes it there, it won't stay forever. Someone will find it and undoubtedly turn it into the authorities. I doubt you want to be trapped on Earth like your sister."

Fietch chuckled lightly. "Let's get you going. Do you have what you need?"

GEMINI

41

Colly nodded. She felt nervous and excited. She took one last quick look out the door. She grunted to herself; more than likely, her last view of Gliese was going to be the dirty back lot of Yellowjackets bar.

Fietch reached up and closed the hatch without saying goodbye. He stepped back and lit a fat cigar. Two or three of his men stepped out of the bar and leaned against the back wall of the bar and watched.

In a millisecond, there was a brilliant flash of light, and the orb was gone. The air seemed to smell like electricity, and everyone's ears popped. By the time Fietch drew his next breath, Colly was light-years away, cruising through the final black hole that would set her into the Earth's atmosphere.

Fietch took a deep breath and shook his head from side to side. The Space Girl was long gone, and he knew she was gone for good. Even the best return orbs were not 100 percent reliable. In Space Girl's case, 5 percent was a stretch.

8

Here I Come! So Sorry. Bobby's Big Plans

THE ORB BURST THROUGH THE FABRIC OF TIME and space to enter Earth's atmosphere over northeast Nepal. Colly immediately started guiding the ship toward its final location just slightly north of New York City.

Her right hand pressed on a glowing pad, and Colly focused on the screen in front of her. A blue light started to flash and Colly knew that meant she was being tracked by something.

"Oh, fuck me," she mumbled under her breath as the orb dropped down to below ten thousand feet and gained speed as it headed west.

Both the North American Aerospace Defense Command (NORAD) and the Search for Extraterrestrial Intelligence (SETI) complexes went on high alert. Every light was blinking at a top secret SETI site located in Texas. The technicians and scientists were scrambling to try to understand what was going on. This was not a drill or an echo return on radar. This was the real deal. Something had just shattered the outer layer of the top-secret dome of surveillance that the US government, along with several NATO allies, had set up to track any possible extraterrestrial interlopers.

General Mark "Big Mac" Wallis burst into the NORAD command center in Cheyenne, Wyoming, and made a beeline to the radar banks in the center of the huge room.

"Are we sure it isn't the Russians or the Chinese?" he asked, loosening his tie and unbuttoning the top button on his dress blues.

"Negative, Sir," the young captain said as he leaned over the radar. "We tracked it coming through the dome. It hit our atmosphere over Nepal and it's heading west. Speed is high subsonic."

General Wallis leaned toward the radar. "Any idea where it might be headed?"

"Negative again, Sir. All we can tell is it's heading west, and it looks like it's a single."

Wallis stood up straight and motioned to his top lieutenant, who obediently walked quickly over to the general's side.

"Lieutenant, get me the president on the horn."

Meanwhile, at Incirlik Air Base in northern Turkey, six F-22 Raptors scrambled to meet Colly as she crashed the sound barrier somewhere over eastern Iran and started her dash west over the Middle East. The F-22s climbed to ten thousand feet and accelerated over Iran to meet the unidentified object.

Colly looked at the screen and saw them heading straight for her.

"Oh! Okay ... *six* of you? Damn," she said with her eyebrows crinkled.

She tapped her hand pad and then tapped the screen twice to show the F-22s. Colly touched the screen two more times and smiled.

"Sorry, boys," she said softly and gently while she tapped the screen lightly six quick times.

Hundreds of miles away, the F-22s' engines flamed out almost at the exact same time. Instantly, the calls for ejection and maydays came screaming over the radios. Six chutes floated down over Iran close to the Caspian Sea. The pilots floated gently downward as they watched their aircrafts explode in six fireballs upon hitting the desert floor.

Just a few hundred feet from the ground, the pilots started adjusting their chutes for landing. They were all instantly distracted as they watched as the orb silently sailed by, gaining speed. What they couldn't see was Colly mouthing, "I'm sorry, you guys!" out the side window of the orb.

She pushed the orb forward at Mach 4 speed and sprinted across the Middle East and Eastern Europe. Her altitude fluctuated from a few hundred feet above the ground, up to thirty thousand feet. She watched as the Earth's defense systems sprang into action. She had to put down several more fighters, but for the most part, they were unable to catch or find her. Skill and luck kept her generally hidden from Earth eyes.

Thousands of miles away, in a little apartment in New York, Bad Bobby Underwood sat in front of his ostentatious wall of ham radios, slack-jawed and bug-eyed.

"Holy fuck," he said, barely able to contain his excitement as he monitored the events unfolding over the Middle East.

This was it. Finally, he'd caught it. Finally, he knew some serious shit was going down. He wrote feverishly as he listened to the chatter coming from SETI, NORAD, and the skies over Iran. He jotted down names and locations and was able to track the UFO headed west over Europe by simply following the top-secret communications and monitoring the activity at air bases strung across Europe and the region.

He listened as US and allied air bases sprung instantly into alert status and fighters scrambled to intercept the strange alien craft. They all seemed to flame out and crash at the same time. The radios screamed, "Mayday!" and desperate calls to eject. The pilots were all trying to give their locations and conditions. Bobby listened and plotted the craft's location the best he could on a digital map on his computer.

He knew the UFO had accelerated greatly over the northern Atlantic and that a US Naval frigate fired an advanced and top-secret surface-to-air missile at the craft. As soon as Colly said, "Poof," smiled, and touched the screen, the missile lost all directional control and landed harmlessly in the north Atlantic.

Bobby paced frantically in his living room. He occasionally sat down in front of the radios and then stood again. His excitement bubbled over.

Like some strange cartoon, a light bulb instantly went off in Bobby's head. What if he could somehow kill the intruder? Take out this alien invader. He envisioned the military holding a lavish ceremony for him while the president pinned the Congressional Medal of Honor on his chest. There would be a parade for him where he rode on a huge float with his foot pinning down the dead alien while the crowds threw flowers and chanted his name.

He would be a hero throughout the world. He imagined all the sweet pussy he would get. The women would practically be begging to get fucked by the great Bobby Underwood, slayer of aliens. Savior of the planet.

He sat at his desk, adjusted his radios, and nervously tapped his feet while he imagined his new mansion on the California coast surrounded by bodyguards. The paparazzi would follow him everywhere, trying to catch a glimpse of the alien hunter. He would finally fulfill his fantasy of fucking two women at once while they fucked each other. His garage would be full of exotic sports cars: Ferrari, Lamborghini, Bugatti. He was sure they would make a movie out of his life. The story of how he was hired by the governments of the world to track down and kill alien life forces that used the Earth as their host. He would be famous and rich—and have all the pussy he wanted.

Bobby pictured franchising his alien-hunter idea. An office in every country. They would come, hat in hand, to ask Bobby Underwood for help. Maybe the US government had advanced spacecraft that he could use to get to other planets to chase aliens. Who knew? One thing he did know: the first step to this amazing future was finding and killing this alien that had decided to invade his own backyard.

9

Hard Landings

COLLY DROPPED THE ORB JUST FEET ABOVE the waves and accelerated to Mach 5 as soon as she hit the halfway point over the north Atlantic. An amazingly huge rooster tail of water exploded behind the orb hundreds of feet into the night sky as she tore across the Atlantic. She piloted the orb so close to the water that weeks later, when the scientists from SETI were taking samples from the craft, they scratched their heads at the fine layer of Earth sea salt on the orb.

The blue light no longer blinked, so Colly knew she was no longer being tracked. She had managed to drop out of sight, but she wasn't sure how long that would last.

She slowed the craft greatly as she started to close in on the North American coast. She pulled back and set the altitude for one thousand feet. She was still going way too fast and gently rolled her fingers across the light pad. The orb slowed to 500 mph and hooked a sweeping left turn over Nova Scotia. Colly laughed and giggled as she rolled the orb and stayed upside down for a brief minute. A hot second later, her busy fingers danced on the light pad, and her altitude dropped quickly.

As she approached the Hudson Valley, New York, she had to smile as she remembered what she had read about the blackouts there in 1965. Little did most Earth people know that a craft from the same system of Gliese was literally running out of energy and figured out it was able to convert electric power from the substations in the valley to charge the navigation system on the craft. This caused a blackout in New York City and the surrounding areas. She smiled at this little nugget of extraterrestrial trivia.

Her fingers continued to dance on the controls as she prepared to land. Her stomach tingled with anticipation and nervousness. She had pre-planned to land the orb north of New York in the hopes of staying as clandestine as possible.

"Oh, shit," she said as she flipped on stealth mode, which darkened the orb and silenced the hum of the reactor. She mentally kicked herself for not doing that earlier. The orb was black and silent while in stealth mode, so no one saw or heard her coming. The only thing that may have tipped off the sparsely populated rural area was the cattle smashing their hooves against the dirt and shaking their heads nervously.

Colly took a deep breath and landed the orb in a small clearing about a mile from the nearest road. No local alarms were raised.

10

Here Comes Colly, Earth. Yuck! Jaguar F-Type

THE THICK NEW YORK WOODS WERE QUIET, except for the sounds of a few evening birds chirping around the motionless orb and the distant, faint sound of a chain saw. With a quick flash, the side of the orb opened, and light poured out onto the darkening forest floor. Very slowly, Colly stuck her head out and looked around curiously. She wore aviator goggles and looked like an incredibly strange and comical version of a throwback space traveler from some old-time Hollywood movie.

She scanned her new surroundings through the goggles and smiled. Earth. Earth. Her hips swung around, and she stepped out. Her six-foot, three-inch frame lurched above the small group of shrubs close to the orb. She reached in, grabbed her pack, and set a timer on the control panel. The timer would all but render the hyper-advanced technology useless to Earth scientists. She knew the orb would probably be discovered eventually, not that she cared. By interrupting the cycle of information from the orb, she could gain valuable time to retreat from the Earth authorities. She did smile when she read the little message that Fietch had written on the inside of the craft. It simply said, "Have fun, Space Girl! Say hi to Buddy Presley for me!" Oh, how she would like to see the look on the faces of the scientists when they read that little piece of script!

There was just enough sunlight left in the day for Colly to navigate her way through the woods around the landing site with relative ease. She pulled out a small map and an earthly compass. She looked left,

49

then right, and then held the compass in her palm, and with a hint of finality, she began to walk east.

With her backpack strapped on and goggles pushed up on her head, she stepped carefully through the wooded landscape. Occasionally, she would bend down and pick up foliage that caught her eye and examine it closely. She headed east through the woods and gazed at the mammoth trees; her mind spun from a variety of plants that seemed to be everywhere. She took deliberate deep breaths and inhaled the sweet forest air. The late-evening sunlight cut through the trees in shadowy strips that threw Colly into an awestruck fog of amazement.

As she stepped lightly across a patch of green moss, out of the corner of her eye, she caught a little creature walking with its young in tow across a massive fallen tree. The little black-and-white creature had a fluffy tail that stuck straight up. Colly tilted her head slightly, crouched down, and smiled.

"Hi, little lady," she whispered. "Are those all your little babies?"

She dropped down on her hands and knees and slowly crawled toward her new little friend. She had never seen such a cute creature! She held her hand out and made kissy noises to try and coax the little cutie closer.

When Colly inched her way to within arm's reach of the little black-and-white creature, it turned around and sprayed her with a disgusting and pungent liquid.

"Oh! *Fuck*! Dammit! Jesus Christ, for fuck!" she screamed, fell backward, and landed on her ass.

"Goddammit! You little shit!" she barked, then spit and coughed. "Ewwwww! What the shit?"

Colly stood up instantly and comically walked in small circles while wiping her face over and over and spitting onto the ground. She tripped and fell backward and landed on her ass with a grunt. Finally, she struggled into her backpack, pulled out a small container, and dripped a small drop of clear liquid into the palm of her hand. She dabbed her face and the pungent liquid and smell disappeared.

"Go fuck yourself," she mumbled and sneered at the little black-and-white creature as it walked away along the log with its children in tow.

No worse for wear after the skunk incident, Colly worked her way through the ever-darkening woods until she came to a slight hill that led to a gravel parking lot. It was getting close to being fully dark now, and she could see lights glowing over the hill. Ever so carefully, she crawled to the top of the hill, comically lowered her goggles, and peeked over. Her eyes shifted from side to side. She could see a parking lot full of strange aero cars and a huge, elegant neon sign that read, "Whitetops Winery." She watched carefully as several well-dressed couples walked hand in hand into the rural establishment, laughing and talking loudly. As the couples opened the door, Colly heard soft violin music drifting out from the restaurant, along with the distant sounds of glasses clinking and toasting.

Her eyes caught a car in the back of the lot that seemed to shine a little brighter than the others. She took one last look around, scrambled over the hill on her hands and knees, and ran across the parking lot. Her shoes skidded in the gravel as she stopped quickly at the car. Her fingers touched it slowly, and Colly grinned with her eyes open wide.

"Jag-u-ar efff type," she whispered in what she perceived as a sexy voice and bit her bottom lip. Her index finger tapped the door handle and the door clicked open.

"Oh, yeah," she said and then tossed her pack on the passenger's seat and climbed in. She tapping the steering wheel and the pearl-white F-type roared to life. Colly squealed and laughed. She tightened up her Earth goggles, and five minutes later, she was speeding toward Manhattan with Rush's "Red Barchetta" blaring on the Jag's car stereo.

11

Hide and Seek.
Big Secrets. Found it!

"WHAT DO YOU MEAN, WE LOST IT? WHAT exactly does that mean?" General Wallis barked at his staff, who were gathered around a large table inside a formal conference room deep inside the Cheyenne bunker in Wyoming. The pink skin of his scalp showed through his buzzed haircut, and behind his left ear was a pronounced mole. Behind the general's back, some of the younger staff members had nicknamed him Corky, as if that cork behind his ear might blow at any time. His chiseled face was tight and a single, bold vein throbbed on his forehead. He had just gotten off the phone with the president, who'd made it very clear that the decorated general needed to find answers.

Wallis was a young and highly decorated general who demanded a lot from his subordinates. For the last seven years, he was in command of a top-secret program code-named Shooting Star. Over the years, he was privileged to the most top-secret information on the planet—possibly in history. He knew for facts what most basement investigators could only hypothesize about. The general knew in intimate detail about the twenty-three species of extraterrestrial life that had visited the planet in the last fifty years. Not all life forms could be trusted 100 percent, but as a general rule of thumb, they were all considered cooperative. Over the years, only one instance of turmoil had rocked the proverbial boat: the abductions in the 1970s had caused a major stir and uproar.

The US government objected vocally when a race of extraterrestrials started a program that involved abducting humans and breeding them with their kind. This program lasted only a short time, and in an above-top-secret meeting in the Nevada desert, the extraterrestrials explained that their breed was slowly becoming extinct and human DNA was a close match, and breeding with humans would ensure the progression and survival of their race. In return for its cooperation, the US government was placated with a prototype engine that could someday be used to travel the solar system, along with a chemical chain that could greatly advance medical programs. Six weeks later, a ship landed in an area of Nevada called Groom Lake, and the seventy-five earthlings that were taken for testing and DNA harvesting were unceremoniously returned.

Shortly after that incident, the Galaxy Control Treaty was created and ratified by all twenty-three of the extraterrestrial groups that had visited Earth in recent history. The GC, as it was called, would be the liaison between Earth and extraterrestrials who had questions or concerns about visitation and other policies.

Wallis's lieutenant, a hard-nosed career man named Bonilla, stood up and spoke firmly.

"Sir, we know it crossed into US territory from Nova Scotia. Local PDs are fielding multiple calls from civilians that saw it."

"What's the cover story?" Wallis growled.

"We're telling the locals and the press it's an SR-71 from NASA that went off course."

Wallis nodded in approval and motioned for the lieutenant to sit down.

"Where was the last reported sighting?" The general lit a cigarette and tossed the now empty pack into the garbage can.

"We have a local PD just north of The Hudson who saw it moving low and slow. Right now, we are betting it's around the Hudson Valley. Air traffic control at JFK, Newark, and LaGuardia couldn't see it, indicating it was probably under five hundred feet." The lieutenant cleared his throat and continued. "We are hypothesizing our new friend is heading into New York. That seems to be the pattern over the years, and there's no reason to think otherwise."

"New York. Fuck," the general said and took a deep drag from his cigarette. "Okay. Let's keep it simple and easy, folks. First things first, get a message out to Galaxy Control and ask if they have any ships on Earth right now. Let's keep the NYPD in line. This is a 'need to know' only, folks. Grab a handful of agents, and let's start poking around in New York. Maybe we'll get lucky and something will shake loose. Get SETI on the horn and see what they can tell us. Ask that kid, Raptis, what he thinks. Tighten up the SR-71 cover story, and someone put a lid on the press. Let's move, people."

Just as his staff began to stand up and shuffle papers, the phone on the table rang twice in quick succession. The general grabbed the phone and held up his hand, signaling for his staff to stay put.

"Wallis. Yes. Yes. When? Okay. Okay. Yes, I will."

Wallis looked at his staff and said, "Okay, people, good news. We have the ship."

12

Let's Dance! Gary's Dirty Little Secret. Mickey D's

WITHIN A SHORT FIFTEEN MINUTES OF COLLY leaving the orb, a teenage hunter and his father stumbled upon the craft and called the local sheriff. The sheriff listened intently to the hunter and rushed out to the site immediately. With flashlights cutting through the woods like laser beams, the fat-bellied sheriff and his slow-witted deputy took one look at the strange craft, scratched their heads, and called the state police, who in turn called the feds.

Within forty-five minutes, a train of feds and agents from the New York field office of the FBI were dispatched and on their way to the crash site from Manhattan in a parade of unmarked sedans.

In his little apartment, a chain-smoking Bobby Underwood was monitoring the entire course of events as they unfolded. He wrote frantically on a scratch pad as the radio chirped and blared information about a craft that landed north of the city. The local sheriff's department was jabbering about aliens and the end of the world. Finally, the sheriff got on the horn and told them all to keep quiet.

"Jesus fucking fuck Christ!" Bobby said frantically as he grabbed his jacket, knife, and car keys. He slammed the door and ran down the steps three at a time. His old Chrysler New Yorker was parked right out in front of his building, thanks to a handicap placard that he'd stolen and put on his rearview mirror. He fired up the old, rusty car and slammed it into drive. The beast belched blue smoke and took off, bald tires squealing, like a bullet from a gun and headed north to the crash site.

Colly glanced down and saw the little light that looked like a gas pump blinking on the Jag's dash. "Ah, shit," she said, surprised. Straight ahead, she saw a Gulf station, and she guided the Jaguar carefully into the lot and up to the pumps.

She got out, studied the gas pumps quizzically for a minute, and quickly figured out how to fuel the car. Just as the car started taking on gallons of high-octane gas, the radio began to play the classic Kiss song, "Strutter." Colly stepped over, opened the door, and turned it way, way up. In an instant, she was dancing like the videos she watched on Earth's *Dance Moves* before she left Gliese. She swung her arms and did all the classic dance moves in the parking lot in front of the pumps. She laughed as she danced ridiculously badly. In front of the station, a small crowd of five or six people began watching her in disbelief. Colly looked at them, nodded, and smiled as she did her best version of the outdated "Macarena" dance. An elderly couple stood wide-eyed and watched this strangely tall and beautiful woman dance so badly. The gentleman shook his head, snickered, and pulled his wife away from the scene. They both laughed as they climbed in their old pickup truck and pulled out of the dirt parking lot in a cloud of dust.

While Colly was jitterbugging, she glanced up and looked behind her and stopped dancing. She watched as five unmarked sedans screamed past the station, one right after the other. Trailing in tow, in an almost comical scene, was Bad Bobby Underwood. His old New Yorker was farting smoke and trying desperately to keep up with the others. Colly saw Bobby's profile, looking serious and staring straight ahead. Both his hands were firmly placed on the steering wheel, and a generic yellow light flashed away on his dash. Colly stifled a giggle as Bobby went by.

Had she been focused on her surroundings and not dancing, she would have sensed the bad man instantly. She would have known who he was and what he looked like. Instead, she was distracted and preoccupied with her new world. This was a mistake that she would regret later.

The car was fueled, and Colly walked into the store. A group of local teenagers leaned against the counter and stared at her while holding bags of chips and candy.

"Ummmmm ... that was some interesting dancing you were doing," the old man behind the counter said to Colly as she walked to the candy aisle. She looked over her shoulder and shot the man a grin.

The teenage boys with the chips snickered and looked away. Colly ignored them for the moment and grabbed a huge handful of candy bars from the shelf. She walked by the boys and looked down at them slyly. The one older alpha boy began to laugh, almost challenging her. She dropped the candy on the counter, reached into her pocket, pulled out four fifty-dollar bills, and dropped them on the register. She snatched the bagged candy and turned around without waiting for change. The boys hid immature smiles as Colly stopped in front of them.

She towered above the alpha boy and craned her neck down toward him, eyes squinted. She raised her index finger, held it up for a brief second, then gently touched the boy's nose and tapped it twice.

The boy gave her a sneer of disgust as Colly turned and started toward the door with her eyebrows raised, as if someone had just told her a juicy secret.

"Fuckin' weirdo fuck," the alpha said and then laughed nervously and looked back and forth at his boys. Colly turned around slowly and smiled gently as she opened the door.

"Now, Gary ..."

The alpha boy's eyes widened. "How the hell do you know my name?" he said and puffed out his chest in a display of adolescent vanity.

"Do you still try on your sister Patty's bra and underwear when everyone leaves for church on Sunday mornings?"

Gary's stomach turned over in panic as the others began laughing hysterically at him. Only Gary knew about his fetish—or so he thought.

At the crash site, a federal agent strung yellow tape around a fifty-foot perimeter while other agents looked into the orb and talked softly to each other. A set of large spotlights were placed around the orb and lit up the entire area. An agent took pictures of the orb and sent them off immediately to command in Colorado. He made sure to get plenty of pictures of the message that was handwritten in the cockpit of the orb.

The ship had skidded to a stop and was semi-buried in the dirt. The craft had missed landing in a creek bed by about fifteen feet. Above, it had hit some branches from an oak tree and snapped them off.

On top of a small rise overlooking the site, Bobby Underwood was looking at the unfolding scene below through a new pair of infrared binoculars. He shook his head in utter disbelief and mumbled, "Fuck," to himself.

He gathered as much information as he could, knowing in an hour this place would be too hot for him to get anywhere nearby. From what he could gather from the radio calls and what he was seeing here, the craft had landed there roughly an hour ago. Apparently, it had broken through the Earth's atmosphere somewhere near Southern China, possibly Nepal. The US response was swift but entirely ineffective against this obviously well-organized and planned pre-invasion.

Yes, it was time for him to step in and do what those clueless fucks couldn't. Time for him to smash the break-in-case-of-emergency alarm box. Time for Bobby Underwood to spring into action and save the world from this scourge of the universe.

He ducked low and slithered away back to his car that was parked on the side of the dirt road. Time to get back to New York and get things going. Time to make history. Those ridiculous feds had no idea what they were doing. Bobby had no doubt that they were completely in the dark and looking for guidance. He would be their savior. Bobby Underwood ... Alien Hunter.

Colly beeped the horn twice and waved at the slack-jawed kids in the station as the Jag roared out of the Gulf station and headed south toward New York City. Colly grabbed the goggles from the passenger seat and put them on. She smashed the accelerator and merged onto the highway. The Jaguar screamed as she ran through the gears. She scarfed on her candy bars from the gas station and was instantly high on the sugar. Of course, Milky Way bars were her new favorite Earth candy. She adjusted the radio and tuned in the local rock-and-roll station. Kiss was singing about rocking and rolling all night and partying every day. Colly bobbed her head, tapped her foot, and tried to sing along, unsuccessfully.

As the rural landscape began to change to suburban and then to urban, Colly slowed the F-type down to legal speeds and began enjoying this strange and odd world.

Following the car's primitive GPS, she took the Cuomo Bridge over the Hudson River and headed south, absorbing everything. She looked around at the growing number of billboards and read them all under her breath.

"Yoooonnkeeerrrrrrs," she said out loud, holding a Butterfinger candy bar in her hand. *What a strange world,* she thought over and over, unaware of the melted chocolate around her mouth.

As she zipped south into Manhattan, the Westside Highway had just light, sporadic traffic this late in the evening, and Colly was able to slalom the Jag easily through traffic. She counted the streets down and looked for her turn. She hooked a sharp left onto Fifty-Ninth Street and overcompensated the turn, badly. The car skidded, fishtailed, and jumped the curb; it bounced into a beauty salon and shattered the salon's windows, sending shampoo and assorted skin-care products rolling out onto the street.

Colly froze, wide-eyed, with her hands on the wheel. After a second, she shouldered the door open and stepped out and surveyed the damage with her hands on her hips.

"Oh, shit," she said, blankly looking around.

She grunted, lifted her goggles, and slid them up on her forehead. A crowd was slowly gathering, attracted by the sound of the crash. She slowly reached in, grabbed her pack, and quickly trotted away toward Eleventh Avenue. None of the New Yorkers thought to follow her. As far as they were concerned, it was just another day in The Big Apple.

The police showed up at the wrecked hair salon a short time later and took statements. The witnesses all had the same description of the car thief: between six-feet and six-feet, five-inches tall; thin; black hair; freckles; oddly clear, blue eyes; and wearing vintage pilot's goggles.

As the local police were finishing up, a pack of feds and FBI agents descended on the scene. They quickly cleared the spectators away and set up portable spotlights that lit up the Jaguar. They cordoned off the block, and several men in protective suits sat in the F-Type holding Geiger counters.

Some of this information would be vaguely shared at the local precinct during the morning roll call. A BOLO would be issued for Colly in all five boroughs.

Just as Colly was smashing up the hair salon on Fifty-Ninth, Bobby was walking into his apartment holding a to-go bag from McDonald's. His mind was racing and spinning, puffing him up with adrenaline. He threw his backpack down and paced the floor, occasionally looking out the window for any signs of feds or aliens.

"Fucking unreal!" He sat down at his desk, opened his bag of food, and scarfed down the soggy fries three at a time.

He immediately flipped on the power switch, and the lines and stacks of radios whirred to life. The chatter across the globe was constant and excitable.

He learned very quickly about the BOLO and who had wrecked the car. He knew it was his target. Why else would the feds be on the scene of a run-of-the-mill car accident? This was it. This was all tied into the incidents upstate. *Yep*, Bobby thought, *this is definitely part of the craft that landed upstate.*

Bobby spent the next hour in front of his radios, chain-smoking and writing down any information he was able to get. His hand worked feverishly as he wrote down locations and notes about what was happening. At one point, he thought about heading up to Fifty-Ninth Street to see the car, but then he thought better of it. By now, they had certainly towed the car, and what information could he possibly gain? No, he was better off here in front of his command center listening to the cross talk of the feds.

Tomorrow was another day, and tomorrow, he would hunt again. He may just hunt more than one bitch. The excitement of the events around him were working him up in more ways than one.

That night, he lay in bed, thinking about his favorite prey. Oh, yes, he would have to make time for two kinds of hunting. His groin felt full and uncomfortable. He closed his eyes and thought about his extracurricular activities. Minutes later, he released copious amounts of sperm into his filthy bedsheets. Tomorrow.

Colly jogged lightly through the streetlight-and-neon-lit catacombs of Manhattan, eventually headed for the Plaza Hotel. From time to time, she would look over her shoulder to make sure she wasn't being followed. She wasn't.

The entire world around her seemed to pulse and vibrate under her feet. Everything was alive and seemed to breathe. She vaguely wondered how hard it was going to be to focus and channel Josi among all this background noise and nonsense. Meh, she would have to cross that complicated bridge when she got to it.

As soon as she took the corner into the heart of Times Square, she let out a little gasp and laughed. "Whoa," she said blankly as she looked up and around.

Her eyes darted everywhere as she tried to absorb this strange and fascinating place. She read all the billboards and ads that seemed to be everywhere. Of course, she had read and seen pictures of this Times Square place, but she wasn't expecting it to be so full of life and so huge. The ground underneath her feet seemed to have a palpable heartbeat.

Over the next hour or so, Colly knocked about the city and looked at the strange sights, sounds, and smells of The Big Apple. She tried to stay in the shadows and keep to herself as much as she could. She made an attempt to blend in as much as possible, but she, like her twin, naturally stuck out in a crowd. She took a cab to Greenwich Village and paid the cabby $200 for the fare.

Eventually, she began to grow tired, and she set her sights on the hotel. She had wandered farther than she thought, and before she realized it, she had drifted down to almost the bottom of Sixth Avenue. She turned abruptly and walked toward the hotel; she gawked at all the amazing sights as she went, and of course, tagged the *C&J* mark.

Sometime later, Colly stood at the front desk of the Plaza Hotel. She looked around and absorbed yet another fascinating place in this odd world. The lobby of the lush and famous hotel was impressive on a level she hadn't really expected. This building, like many of the others, Colly examined with her engineer eyes and nodded in silent approval. She was impressed at the design and construction of many of the city's fine buildings.

She sighed tiredly as her eyes locked and focused on the cute girl who was just finishing taking reservations from an older couple at the other end of the counter. Colly's eyebrow instantly raised curiously. The girl's name tag was perfectly positioned on her white blouse and read boldly: "Carrie."

Colly whispered, "Carrrriee."

Carrie glanced up and saw Colly standing at the counter. She looked twice at her and stumbled a little on her way to the reservation computer in front of Colly.

"Hello. How can I help you?" the cute girl, Carrie, choked out with a nervous smile.

Colly narrowed her pale-blue eyes just slightly and said, "Hello, Carrie. My name is Colly, and I have a hotel reservation, please."

"Ummmm ... okay ... okay ...," Carrie replied and began typing. As she typed, she stole glances at Colly, flustered by this unusual beauty.

"Here we go ... Colly. Th ... three nights in a suite."

Colly nodded and bounced on her heels a few times while reaching in her bag for her American Express card.

She slid the card across the counter. "Will this do, I hope?"

"Okay. Yes, it certainly will. Thank you ... okay ... " Carrie stumbled over her words.

As Carrie nervously ran the card through the machine, Colly got a mischievous, bent smile on her face and gently blew a small, sweet breath toward the cute girl. She bit her lip and waited. Carrie stopped, let out a choppy breath, and crossed her legs.

Colly smiled and asked, "Are you okay?"

Carrie squeezed her eyes tight and nodded quickly.

Colly leaned into the girl as if she was going to kiss her. Carrie froze in nervous shock as Colly raised her index finger carefully, leaned over the counter, and playfully gave a little tug to her earlobe.

"Nice," she said and smiled.

It wasn't until after Colly had left the front desk and headed toward the bank of elevators that Carrie realized her panties were completely wet with her slick fluid. With a quick gasp of wide-eyed realization, it hit her that this strange girl, who would be the center of her sexual fantasies for months, had just made her orgasm.

Colly walked into the suite behind the bellhop and scanned the huge room with wide eyes and an open mouth. The bellhop showed her around politely and pointed out all the amenities, then stood by the door waiting for a tip. Colly caught on and hurriedly pulled out a small

handful of fifty-dollar bills and gave them to the young man. He stood
at the door and looked down at his hand and up at Colly, then back at his
hand, his mouth hanging agape. Colly smiled, nodded her head quickly,
and slammed the door in his face without saying anything.

She tossed her bag on the big bed and walked around the room
looking into and around everything. She peered into everything
like a curious child might. At one point, she was on her hands and
knees closely examining the plumbing under the bathroom sink. She
opened the bottom drawer on the vanity and pulled out the hair dryer,
examined it closely, and took it with her into the living room. She tossed
it on the bed nonchalantly. The room had a huge set of windows that
covered the entire wall of the suite. Colly stood there and looked over
the nighttime cityscape in awe. As many times as she had looked at
photographs of the great metropolis New York, she was taken aback by
its urban beauty and size.

Somewhere out there was her sister, Josi. Somewhere.

The shower took some quick figuring out, but eventually, she
managed to tone the water perfectly. She kept comically sticking her
head out the curtain and looking around because she constantly kept
thinking she heard something. Later, she would attribute that to simple
nervousness. Standing naked in the shower on a strange planet twenty-
plus light-years from home will do that to a girl.

As bedtime slipped in, Colly wrapped herself up in a huge, fluffy,
white blanket with the lights out and the TV on. She had ordered some
food from the kitchen downstairs and nibbled at it slowly. In a small
glass bottle was a substance that looked like little grains of white sand.
Colly shook out a little smidge and slowly put it on her tongue. She
smacked her lips quickly and shrugged. This strange-tasting seasoning,
which was nonexistent on Gliese, was to become a fast and constant
staple of Colly's Earth diet.

Sitting cross-legged on the bed with the blanket covering everything
but her eyes, she resembled a strange, intergalactic snowman. She was
watching the classic film *Close Encounters of the Third Kind* on cable,

and she wasn't sure if this is what earthlings thought extraterrestrial beings were really like. There were certain parts of the movie where she raised her eyebrows and thought to herself, *Yep, that's kinda close, I guess.*

Soon, she tipped over and fell into sweet, dreamless sleep.

13

Josi Takes a Stroll.
The Bump

JOSI STOOD ON THE CROWDED SUBWAY
platform below Forty-Fourth Street early on Saturday morning. What she didn't realize was that twenty light-years away, her twin sister, her Gemini, was preparing to travel across the universe to find her.

Many of the tourists and locals openly eyed her on the platform without trying to be rude. Occasionally, she would shoot them a little grin or a quick wink, which they always seemed to like. They acted as if a celebrity had just smiled and acknowledged them, even if it was just a small gesture.

She was dressed in casual attire for her day of looking around the city: skinny jeans and an oversized black hoodie that had a New York Yankees logo on the front in big, bold, white font. The hoodie was accented by a pair of black Converse high tops with purple laces. Her stark-white hair flowed out from under a black stocking cap that was embroidered with a bold number 2 in a circle—Derek Jeter, the famous Yankee shortstop's number. Her eyes, facial features, and freckles stood out in stark contrast to the black sweatshirt and cap, making her almost impossible not to stare at.

Last night's dream continued to haunt, excite, and perplex her. The Zon rolling across the bedroom floor solidified her belief that what was happening was indeed real and not some fictitious illusion. No, this was real, and almost minute by minute, the fog that had clouded her mind for most of her life was being brushed away and she could start to see little spots of blue sky. Yes, she was becoming sharper, and her focus now centered on finding her sister, Colly, and getting home to Gliese.

She knew Colly was here in New York, or would be here shortly. She just *knew*. She could feel her presence like one might smell the rain hours before it begins. She could *smell* her twin coming. Her senses were changing almost by the minute and things were becoming more acute, sharp like a razor blade.

Her entire life, she'd known there was something different about how she perceived things, and the older she got, the more pronounced it was becoming. But now—it was accelerating at an alarming rate.

When she took a deep breath and focused, it was as if everything around her was in technicolor and dripped secret information from every crack. It wasn't a terribly unpleasant feeling at all, and the information she was able to see came to her in soft edges, not harsh realities or jagged little edges.

She knew Colly was looking for her, like she was looking for Colly, and they would find each other sooner or later. This, she was sure.

There also seemed to be a rift in the otherwise smooth lines that she and her sister were slowly drawing together. A bump, you might say. *The* Bump. Something that was off and tilted in her new world, and she couldn't quite figure out why she was able to sense this rift so clearly. This other strange presence seemed to be more pronounced as the hours ticked by. The Bump. Something that was flawed and for some reason focused on them. The Bump. Something that was spoiled and rotten. Something that was filled with maggots and worms that could only be seen if you cut it open and let the filth spill out on the street. The Bump. She knew there was nothing she could do about the rift right now. Right now, she needed to focus on the task at hand, which was preparing for Colly.

The train pulled into the platform and the subway door slid open. Josi stepped in and found a seat toward the back of the crowded car.

The train rocked forward, and she closed her eyes and smiled. Maybe today was the day. Would she meet her sister? There was no set path she wanted to follow to find her, but something inside her told her she needed to move quickly and use her mind as well as her feet to find her twin.

After she got off the train, she trotted up the station stairs to the street and made her way down to Battery Park, where she started to walk in a simple hodgepodge of directions. She dodged the thousands of tourists and kept her eyes and mind peeled. Every block, she would focus and call out for Colly in her head as she walked. In a city of almost nine million, she doubted very much she was just going to run into her by chance. No, she would have to work a bit.

Of course, every two or three blocks, she would look over her shoulder and quickly draw the little message *C&J* on the side of a building or on the sidewalk. She constantly scanned the buildings for some trace of Colly. She hoped that sooner or later, she would start to see a message from her sister.

Josi spent the day walking around the city, slowly making her way back and forth and up and down lower Manhattan. Block after block, she called for Colly. Once or twice, she stopped dead in her tracks, while people walked around her on the sidewalk. She heard an oh, so slight voice coming from somewhere. She shut her eyes and called back desperately. No response, so Josi continued to walk and look throughout the day. Chalk in hand.

14

Bad Bobby Does Bad Things. Sad Josi

BAD BOBBY SAT ON THE BENCH IN WASHINGTON Square Park directly across from the fountain, his eyes shifting back and forth like a snake. He swam in his oversized army jacket, which he'd found at a secondhand shop on Canal Street two years ago. It was a little warm for such a coat, but Bobby didn't seem to notice, or care. In his right-hand pocket, he had his hand on a large pocket knife that he had also found on lower Canal Street.

A young couple walked in front of Bobby, hand-in-hand. They smiled and laughed, while bouncing inside jokes off each other. They seemed to be very much in love. He gripped his knife and thought to himself, *You look at me wrong and I'll fuckin' gut ya, motherfuckers! Cunts!*

His mood was dark and frustrated today. He hadn't been sleeping much, and he had been calling off at his job. He knew the alien bitch was in the city, and he was desperately trying to piece together the little treasures and nuggets of information he was gathering from the local police, the feds, and his friends around the world via his array of shortwave radios, police scanners, and hacked frequencies.

So far, Bobby knew she was here in New York. She had landed somewhere south of the Hudson Valley. She stole a Jaguar F-Type, and she was strikingly tall with black hair. Bobby also knew that there was a vague APB out in all five boroughs and New Jersey for her. He scoffed at the thought of such a silly and vague APB. *A tall girl with black hair? Are you fucking serious? That described half the cunts in New York.*

He knew he would find her; after all, she had to sleep and eat, didn't she? That meant she was probably at a hotel in the city. Reason told him that she would be trying to fit into New York culture as much as she could, but it would be difficult for her to hide for long.

Night was settling in, and Bobby had been on the bench for several hours, thinking and scheming. The streetlights flickered on, and the neon lights on Fifth Avenue glowed clearly. The sound of a bluesy saxophone drifted through the park while a group of kids did tricks on their skateboards behind him.

In between his thoughts of the alien, he watched the young, female NYU students walking by. Bobby was fishing, in a way. He watched hundreds of young girls walk by, but none seemed quite right. Not yet, anyway. Finally, a strawberry-blond girl with a green backpack and a sweatshirt with a picture of a peace symbol on it walked by. She was lost in her own world, with her head down and her fingers texting quickly. He eyed the earbuds and he knew she would never hear him coming. He stood up, stretched, and followed the girl toward the darkened streets just outside NYU. Bobby was sure another pair of ripped panties was going to be added to his ever-growing collection.

Just as Bobby stood up to follow the cute strawberry-blond NYU student, Josi was being seated at the Waverly Diner on Sixth Avenue, a few blocks away. She had spent the day walking around lower Manhattan, looking and feeling for Colly. It hit her all at once that she hadn't eaten anything since the two bowls of Frankenberry this morning, so she ducked into the diner for some much-needed food.

The waitress poured her a cup of coffee, smiled, and handed her a menu. Josi took a quick look at the menu and set it aside. From her booth, she had a clear shot of the street and the building across the way. As she stirred her coffee and carefully took a sip of hot brew, her eyes lifted, and she froze instantly in mid-sip. Across the street was a Starbucks, and written on the building's facade in new, bold, white chalk was the tag *C&J*.

Josi smiled slightly and bit her lip. "I'll be dipped in shit," she muttered in reserved disbelief. Apparently, her sister had been hanging around Sixth Avenue in Greenwich Village recently.

Under the *C&J* tag was an arrow pointed up Sixth Avenue. At the end of the arrow was a little heart. She shook her head and smiled. She stared at the tag for a long time. Eventually, the waitress nudged her.

"You okay, doll?" she asked Josi.

"Ummm. Yeah, yeah. I'm fine. Can I have a grilled cheese with fries, a side of ranch dressing, and a chocolate coke, please?" she asked and handed the menu back to the gum-popping waitress.

The waitress hurried away to place the order, and in that instant, Josi started to feel nervous. Her excitement of seeing the tag from her sister faded away all at once. Her palms started to feel tingly, and she knew something was off center. She breathed deep and closed her eyes. The diner noises seemed to fade away entirely as she drifted away.

It was The Bump. He was close, frighteningly close. She felt like she was falling forward into a distant void. In that instant, she was in a blurry world that was coming into soft focus. Her body was still at the diner, but her mind was blocks away. She felt like she was floating, and she could see a dark and dirty alley. Dumpsters overflowed with garbage, and several cats jumped from the top of one dumpster to another. Their meows echoed and floated through the alley. Rats scurried behind the piles of garbage and made little squeaking noises. The sounds of the city were distant but rang clear through the alley. She could hear a cry from a girl and the sounds of a struggle. Josi wasn't sure how she knew, but the girl's name was Tabatha, and she had a little brother named Pete. She attended NYU and was studying marketing. She also loved Fleetwood Mac and had broken her right collarbone playing volleyball when she was in the eighth grade. She also knew the shy girl, Tabatha, was a virgin.

From above the dark alley, she could see The Bump. His face wasn't clear, but she could see his green army jacket. He had Tabatha pinned down in a dirty puddle of garbage water that had leaked out of the dumpster. She could see his arm raise up and come down as he smacked and punched her across the face repeatedly in slow, deliberate blows. He knocked out two of her teeth, broke her nose, and split her lip open in two places.

Josi tried to push down to help her, but in this dream-like state, she was unable to move. She tried to scream, but she couldn't. Her voice froze every time she tried. The Bump tore off the girl's pants, and Josi watched him tear off her white panties and stuff them into the pocket of his army jacket. Tabatha screamed in vain under The Bump's hand as he covered her mouth and raped her. Josi watched helplessly in terror and anger.

When The Bump was finished, he stood up, buttoned his pants, and walked over to the dumpster to catch his choppy breath. Tabatha lay in the filth of the alley, sniffling and softly crying, unable to move. Her arm was broken, and her vagina burned, bled, and ached. Bobby grabbed a dirty beer bottle from behind the dumpster and walked back to her. He put his knee across her chest as Tabatha moaned and cried. Bobby twisted and worked the beer bottle into her vagina. She moaned softly and weakly, "No, no, no." He stood up, swung his leg back slowly like a pendulum, and kicked the bottle into her. She gasped, wide-eyed, and passed out from shock and pain. Bobby smugly stared down at her for a long minute. He reached his hand into his oversized pocket and felt the knife. Should he kill her? Why not? She had served her purpose to him, and she was as useless as the rest of them.

In the end, Bobby spared her life. Murder was still out of his league for now, but it was definitely on his bucket list. Instead, he leaned over her and put his knee across her chest again. He slowly and deliberately dipped and swirled his middle and index fingers in an oily, pungent mix of used fryer grease leaking out of the bottom of the dumpster that had pooled into a puddle about the size of a frisbee. Bobby snickered as he slid those two fingers in her rectum.

"No," she cried softly. Her head was dizzy and cloudy, and she tried in vain to move.

Her head shook slowly from side to side as he worked both his oily, disgusting fingers inside her.

Josi shut her eyes, unable to watch as The Bump's arm began to quickly move up and down while Tabatha sobbed and wept.

"Sweetie?" The waitress tugged on Josi's arm. "Everything okay, sweetie pie?"

"No. No. No, it's not!" Josi said and looked around, wide-eyed. She jumped up, grabbed her bag, and ran out of the diner and up Sixth Avenue, toward Hell's Kitchen. She cried and ran with her arms swinging wildly, wishing desperately for her sister to find her so they could find and help the girl, Tabatha.

She ducked into a little doorway off the avenue and threw up behind a trash can. The air felt thick and sticky as she sat on the stoop of an apartment building and tried to catch her breath.

"Oh, Colly. Where are you?" she wondered desperately.

15

Searching. C&J

LATER THAT NIGHT, JOSI WAS COCOONED IN her big bed and cried softly. She wasn't even sure if what she had seen was real, but her new, sharpened instincts told her that it was. She kept hearing the cries of Tabatha as the bottle got kicked into her and seeing Bobby's elbow in the air with his fingers inside her.

Slowly, ever so slowly, Josi began to turn that shock and fear into anger. She knew The Bump was looking for her and Colly, but she had yet to figure out *why* he wanted to find them or even how he was aware of them. Obviously, he was an extremely dangerous man who had a broken mind.

She wiped away a tear and was starting to realize that perhaps *she* was now a dangerous girl. As much as The Bump was looking for her and Colly, she was starting to understand that for him, that might be a very, very bad idea. Although she had yet to meet her sister, she suspected that Colly would not take well to The Bump. God help him if they crossed paths.

Josi got up the next morning feeling sick and upset. She took a hot shower and felt a little better. She tried to put the incidents of last night behind her and make some kind of rough plan to find her sister today. She felt like today might be the day. Her heart raced a little faster than usual and she just felt … close.

Just as she was walking out the door, she stopped and paused. The Zon. She walked back and scooted into the bedroom. On her left was a chest of drawers that held all her clothes and a few sentimental items from her parents. She opened the middle drawer, where the Zon sat by itself in a little dish. She scooped it up and put it in her front pocket. As she was getting ready to close the drawer, she paused, reached back into the drawer, and pulled out an old picture of her with her mom and dad. It was taken at her high school graduation, and all three of them smiled grandly for the camera. She felt a slight sting of tears and put the picture in her back pocket. She wasn't sure why she felt the need to take this piece of her past with her, but she did.

Ten minutes later, she was walking up Ninth Avenue, looking for any sign of her sister. So far, the morning had been relatively uneventful for Josi. More than once, she started to feel discouraged and defeated. Her eyes scanned the huge crowds of people on the avenues, as well as the sparsely occupied side streets. She would stop and sit on a bench and scan the people as they walked by. She felt the people for any kind of hint that Colly was close. Strangely, from time to time, she would feel a slight tingle from someone as they walked by. If she focused on them, she could vaguely feel her sister. Perhaps they had bumped into Colly or had some type of interaction with her.

Occasionally, she would mark her path with the C&J tag in the hopes that Colly would see it and focus in on her. When she stopped for lunch, she got a table on the patio of Gigi Cafe and continued to scan the street.

As the day went on, she was almost starting to feel panicky at the lack of progress she was making. She walked quickly up Ninth and passed Fiftieth, Fifty-Second, Fifty-Third, and upward.

Somewhere around Ninety-First, she started to feel as if her spine was tingling, and somewhere in the recesses of her mind, she felt something like an audible click. She trotted lightly over Eighth Avenue and made her way through the park, dodging cyclists and joggers along the way.

Once she got to Fifth Avenue and Ninety-Seventh, her knees got weak and she knew. She just knew. Colly was close.

16

It's Nice to Finally Meet You. Dismantled. Take Me Home

COLLY WAS ON THE NORTH END OF CENTRAL Park, standing on the corner of Fifth Avenue and 103rd Street and looking around. Throngs of people walked around her, and a few stared up at her and giggled in semi-awe. Colly looked down and curled her lip at a few of the children who were staring.

"Some Earth people should refrain from breeding," she mumbled under her breath while looking over her shoulder.

She had gotten up early that morning and ordered a huge breakfast from room service. She ate ravenously and was amazed at the wonderful and seemingly exotic food that the hotel had sent her. After breakfast, she dressed while watching *The Price is Right* on the television. More than once, she stopped dressing and sat on the end of the bed, clad in her bra and underwear, enthralled with the show. She was comically trying to figure out what was happening and what the point of the show was. She hollered at the television when she disagreed with the contestants. Finally, when the show was over and the local New York news came on, Colly stood there half-dressed and watched. They mentioned a car crash on the west side last night and showed a picture of the wrecked F-type. Colly covered her mouth; her eyes widened and she started laughing.

Just before lunch, she stepped out of the hotel and started to walk down Fifth Avenue. After she made it to Fifty-Fifth Street, she cut over and started tagging conspicuous buildings and locations. She constantly focused and felt for Josi. She got nothing.

Her curiosity was piqued as she stood in front of the Engine 8 Fire Station on Fifty-First Street with her arms hanging down on her sides. Hanging out of the corner of her mouth was a mostly sucked Charms lollipop. The huge red fire truck sat idle and cold in front of her, parked in its stable waiting for a fire call. Colly tilted her head and stepped close to the truck. She touched the bumper of the big red machine with the tip of her finger. All at once, the red lights turned on, the siren started wailing, and the headlights flashed. Colly's eyes lit up, and she clapped and laughed. Three of the station's burly firemen ran out from the back room, jumped into the cab, and turned off the lights and siren. Colly's lips pouted, and she sighed and walked away. The firemen watched her hips sway as she sauntered away down Fifty-First.

She spent the rest of her afternoon looking and tagging. As the afternoon ticked on, she started to feel like she might be getting close. From time to time, her head would tingle and her palms would tighten up. She was getting close. *Soon, Josi ... soon.*

By late in the afternoon, Colly was feeling restless and aggressive. She was close. Oh, so close. As the minutes and hours ticked away, she knew her sister was closing in on her. Or was it the other way around? She knew Josi was nearby, and she suspected that Josi was feeling the same strange vibe. She crossed Fifth Avenue and headed into the park. She bent down and wrote *C&J* on the side of the high-end apartment building; she bit her lip and smiled. The bright tag stuck out like a sore thumb.

Just as she was crossing the street, a horse-drawn carriage lumbered by, clipping and clopping. Colly stopped in her tracks, amazed at the horse and the elaborate carriage it was pulling.

"Oh, my," she said and smiled. She had never seen such a sight! *What a beautiful animal!* she thought to herself. *Not like that little black-and-white fucker that sprayed that gross shit in my face.*

A Yellow Cab's horn blared, and Colly jumped and ran across the street. As she bounced up onto the sidewalk, she called for Josi in her head yet again, and for the first time, she heard Josi call back clearly. Her hands immediately covered her face in gleeful surprise.

Josi! Josi! Are you there? Where are you? Tell me! she thought, loudly and clearly.

Colly! Colly! I'm here, Colly! South … south side of the big park! Colly, I'm on the south side of Central Park!

Colly comically and frantically looked around and turned in circles with her long arms spread out. She got her bearings and ran into the park; she hooked left and jogged south through the park.

Josi, I'm coming!

Colly instinctively found the center of the park and headed straight down. She called out to her sister the entire time. Her head buzzed, and with every step, Josi sounded more clear and more real. Finally, she stopped calling Josi in her head and started calling her with her voice.

"Josi!" she screamed while she ran south down the middle of Central Park, her head turning from side to side.

On Ninety-Seventh Street, Josi began a light trot through pedestrian traffic that was heading out of the park. She cut down the Ninety-Seventh Street Transverse and turned right to head up through the North Meadow.

Colly! she thought loudly. *Colly! I'm coming, Colly!*

She jogged and lightly scanned everything as she looked for her Gemini. Finally, like Colly, she quit calling her sister in her head and began screaming for her with her voice.

"Colly," she choked out tearfully.

They both ran straight toward each other on the North Meadow. Josi saw Colly first and skidded; she fell to her knees and cried.

"Oh, Colly!" she cried out and waved while on her knees.

She stayed on her knees with her arms stretched out as Colly sprinted to her, crying as well. Colly leaped and tackled Josi, knocking her off her knees and onto her back. They both laughed and cried on the grass. They hugged and cried and touched each other's faces as if they couldn't believe the other actually existed.

"Your hair is so black!" Josi said, sniffling and crying as she ran her fingers through it.

"And yours is white!" Colly exclaimed.

"Our freckles! They're the same! Our faces! My God, Colly!"

They instinctively moved nose to nose and gave what looked like Eskimo kisses to each other. Not even the girls knew this was an instinct that Star Children were born with. They each had tiny swirls that created a galaxy of constant circular motion in their eyes. This was another trademark of the Gliesen race that very few of its people had. The elders and the council knew it was the sign of a great and ancient warrior tribe that had long gone extinct. Very few people had The Eyes of God; they were direct descendants of the warrior tribe. The girls also failed to grasp the significance that every freckle on their face was the same. The elders also knew that the freckles on a warrior's face were a star map to their destiny.

The sisters stood up and hugged for a long minute and then stepped back and looked each other up and down with finality. They smiled huge and hugged again.

Ten minutes later, the sisters walked hand in hand through the park on their way back to the Plaza Hotel, where they could rest and talk about perhaps leaving Earth tomorrow. It was now impossible to walk around anywhere without people staring at them.

Colly found this far more amusing and fun than Josi. As they walked through the park, Colly would sometimes make faces at the children who stared in wide-eyed awe. Josi nudged her and laughing and asked her to please stop. When they got close to the Plaza Hotel on Fifty-Ninth Street, a few people with cell phones started snapping pictures. They were sure that the two tall and beautiful twins walking into the famous Plaza Hotel must be mega celebrities of some type. Rather quickly, a crowd gathered to see what all the fuss was about. Josi and Colly ducked inside the lobby of the hotel quickly as security stopped the gawkers and onlookers.

Outside the Plaza, a New York City police officer stood on the corner, drinking a cup of coffee and scanning the throngs of people.

He watched the girls come out of the park and walk into the Plaza. Something about the black-haired girl drew his suspicions. He thought back to roll call yesterday and remembered something about a tall, black-haired woman with freckles crashing a stolen Jaguar into a hair salon on the west side. The description was vague, and New York had more than one woman that fit that description. Nevertheless, he opened his notebook and made a quick note to ask his watch commander about the incident. Underneath his notes, he scribbled, "Plaza Hotel."

Inside the hotel, the girls walked past the front desk, and the cute girl, Carrie, was just starting her afternoon shift. Her jaw dropped and she let out a small gasp as Colly and Josi walked past toward the elevators. Colly turned, looked over her shoulder, and held up her index finger. She mouthed, "Hi," and winked seductively at her.

As soon as the twins opened the door to the suite, Josi covered her mouth with her hand to hold in a laugh. Colly had taken apart most everything in the room that was electric. She stood in the door, astonished, and looked at the microwave that was completely disassembled and at all the parts that were neatly laid out on the floor. The overly complicated toaster oven was also neatly dismantled and spread out on the windowsill. In the bathroom, Colly had also taken apart the hair dryer and the digital scale.

"Colly! What the fuck?" she asked, laughing. "I don't even want to know why!"

Colly smiled and shrugged.

The girls decided to order food from room service instead of going out for dinner. They needed to talk and could not risk anyone eavesdropping on their private conversation. They ordered an abundance of food. They had Colly's Amex card on file, and it, of course, had no limit. A half hour later, there was a knock at the door, and both Josi and Colly shot up and ran to the door, laughing. Josi pushed Colly back with a huge shove.

"I'll get it! I'm guessing you don't know about tipping," Josi said, holding Colly back with her forearm.

Josi opened the door and greeted the impeccable staff member politely while Colly tried to peek around Josi to see what was happening in the hall. The entire scene played out comically as the staff member handed Josi the covered plates.

As they sat eating, they took turns asking questions. Josi touched briefly on Bad Bobby Underwood and told her an abridged version of what she had seen in the alley. Colly assured her that killing Bobby was not only the best thing to do, but the only thing to do, if the opportunity presented itself. Josi tried to explain that murder was wrong on Earth and you could get into trouble for it. Big trouble. Colly shook her head and dismissed the statement.

"Josi, Earth might think killing that animal is wrong, but the rest of the universe thinks it's right. Now, you tell me, whose law is just? Earth law, or the law of a billion other civilizations?"

Josi shrugged and reluctantly agreed with her sister. In the end, Colly stood fast on the idea that sooner or later, one way or another, Bad Bobby would answer for his crimes.

Most of the other topics were fun and light-hearted, and Colly gave Josi a crash course on Gliese life and what to expect. Josi, of course, drilled her with a thousand excited questions. Colly was also interested in her sister's primitive life on Earth.

"Do you live near here? By the hotel?" Colly asked while trying to open a bottle of Grape Crush.

Josi grabbed the bottle out of her hand and gave the cap a gentle twist. Colly seemed intrigued at the little hiss that came out of the bottle.

"No ... well, yes, I guess. I live in a neighborhood called Hell's Kitchen. It's not that far. You can walk to it, but the train or cab is quicker, obviously."

Colly took a swig of the grape soda and started to laugh. She swallowed hard and gasped. "It's all fizzy-feeling in my mouth!"

Josi smiled. "Soooo ... what's your thought on Earth? Do you like it? Is it what you thought it would be?"

Colly shrugged. "It seems like a nice place to visit, but I sure as fuck wouldn't want to live here! Everyone seems to be in such a hurry. The funny part is none of them seem to be going anywhere specific. It's like they are all rushing around in strange circles." The girls laughed, and at that moment, they realized they had the same laugh, too.

Josi reached across the table and held Colly's hands.

"I need to know why I can do all these things. You know, see into people and understand things that I never could before."

"Oh ... that," Colly said and smiled slyly. "That, my sweet sister, is called Blush."

Josi looked confused.

"Look, Josi, it's a rare gift even at home on Gliese. Not everyone can do it. Shit ... not everyone believes it's even real. Back home, most people scoff at it and say it's just an old magic trick. I'm not sure about you, but for me, it either works great or not at all. The older I get, the more it seems to develop. Is it the same for you?"

Josi nodded, agreeing with her Gemini.

"It's just that back home it isn't as ... potent as it is here. It's more subtle. You never noticed this before?"

Josi shook her head. "No. Not really. I guess you could say I had a hint of it growing up, but it really wasn't until you got here that I could do these things."

Colly raised her eyebrows. "Interesting. Oh, and when you were a little girl and you thought the stars were talking to you? That was me."

Josi smiled and whispered, "Kissy for my Sissy. I remember."

Finally, Josi asked the question that Colly had been expecting, and she was frankly surprised it hadn't come sooner.

"Where are our parents?" Josi asked blankly.

Colly stood up and looked out the window. The bottle of Grape Crush hung loosely in her hand. The sun was just starting to set over the buildings that lined the west side of the park. After a brief pause, Colly drew a deep breath and held out her arms.

"Josi, our mom is dead. I'm sorry; she died about the time we were born. I don't know what happened to her, other than she died here. Either on Earth or in this solar system."

She folded her arms across her chest and continued. "I'm not sure how I was able to get home and you had to stay here. We will probably never know. The Hall of Records on Gliese has almost nothing on her, other than that she was a great star warrior and space traveler."

"What was her name?" Josi sighed, teary-eyed.

"Her name? Her name was Calista," Colly said resolutely and smiled.

"And our father?" Josi asked.

Colly shrugged.

"I don't know, Josi. Maybe nobody does. But we have each other now, Josi, and that's all we need." Colly plopped back down on the bed.

They held hands, and Josi looked into Colly's eyes and started to sniffle.

"I love you, and we do have each other. Colly, you came all the way across the universe to get me."

Josi looked up and tried to keep the tears from spilling out.

"You risked your life to find me. You traveled light-years, and you weren't even sure I was here. You saved me with your faith in us. Colly, you're my sister; you're my Gemini. I will follow you to the end of the universe."

Colly looked down and took a deep breath. Two tears ran down her cheeks.

"Josi ... listen carefully to me. It's not that easy, and it's not that simple. Me getting here was the safe part, but getting us home ... not quite so simple or safe."

Josi looked at her, confused, and nervously leaned into her as she anticipated the rest of her story.

"I set an orb to come get us. The window for us to be there to meet it is big, but that's not the problem. The problem is there is just an infinitesimal chance it will be able to lock on to the location I programmed into the system."

"How small of a chance?"

"Five percent." Colly shrugged and looked away.

Josi let out a soft moan and covered her face with her hands.

"Colly! Why didn't you tell me this right away?" Josi threw her hands in her hair.

"I was afraid to tell you! If I was able to find a pilot to fly a ship here, it would be different, but nobody in their right mind would do that, not even friends or family!" Colly continued, almost desperately, her voice rising.

"I tried to get permission to come here from the Gliese Council. They denied me! They have no idea I am here, so if that orb doesn't show up, I will be stuck here, and so will you!"

Colly stood up and started pacing the floor. She looked at Josi and sighed. "Josi ... 5 percent is better than nothing. I had to try, Josi. I had to. Tell me you understand!"

"I understand," Josi said, nodding lightly, wiping away the tears.

They looked at each other and both started to laugh sadly, resigned to what fate may come. Finally, the sisters hugged and gazed out the window high above the busy Manhattan streets. These two Geminis, whose future was still unclear, were now inseparable.

Josi went into the bathroom to shower before they went to bed. When she came out wrapped up in a towel, Colly was sitting on the bed in front of the TV, watching old reruns of *The Six Million Dollar Man*.

"I sure as hell wish I had a hair dryer," Josi said. She rolled her eyes and shook her head back and forth to try to shake off the water. She looked around the suite and mumbled under her breath, "Well, at least the TV is still in one piece."

"This man, is he really worth $6 million?" Colly asked without turning around.

"No, I don't think so. It's an old show. Kinda silly, actually. What else is on?" Josi asked and sighed.

Colly started flipping through the stations slowly, stopping at the movie *Saturday Night Fever.*

"What's this?" she asked Josi.

Josi looked up and chuckled.

"It's a movie called *Saturday Night Fever,*" Josi said and shook her head again. "We can watch that. Can I borrow some clothes to sleep in? Do you have a pair of underwear I can borrow?"

Colly giggled and pointed over her shoulder to her bag. On the television, John Travolta was dancing away, and Colly seemed to find this strangely whimsical.

"Josi, look at this guy dancing! Look at him move his hips. He sure is dapper."

"Dapper?" Josi asked. She smiled and raised her eyebrows.

"Yeah, you know, slick, cute, handsome, sexxxxyyyyy."

Josi nodded while she slipped on a pair of Colly's underwear and a T-shirt she found in Colly's bag.

"Okay, so he's dapper," Josi said as she laughed and adjusted her underwear.

The rest of the night, the girls ate popcorn and watched movies. They ordered ice cream from room service, and Colly tipped the bellhop $200. Josi told her about being a teacher, baseball, and her adoptive parents, while Colly explained how she wasn't adopted until she was fourteen years old but she still managed to go to university and how she designed buildings and that some were famous all over Gliese.

As the girls were getting ready for bed, Josi smiled and said, "I got the Zon, by the way."

Colly continued pulling the sheets back and fluffing the pillows. "I know. In our dream, you said you loved it; I hope you really do."

Josi smiled. "I love it, Sis."

Even though the suite had two king-size beds, the sisters slept in the same bed, close to one another, hand in hand. They lay there in the dark, laughing and talking like teenagers. Eventually, they found sweet, dreamless sleep.

It was sometime just before dawn when Colly awoke to see Josi sitting by the window, looking out into the waking city. The room was quiet except for the ambient noise of the city, which was muted so high up. Colly sat up on her elbows.

"Josi, are you okay? What's wrong?"

Josi turned to her, and even in the dimly lit suite, Colly could see she was upset and concerned.

Colly slid out of bed and walked over to her. She sat next to her and put her arm on her shoulders. Their heads knocked softly together as they sat and looked out the window at the slowly rising sun that was just now peeking over the buildings.

Josi took a deep, choppy breath. "I want to go home."

"Today, Josi. You'll be home today."

17

Bobby Underwood, Junior Detective. Yankees, Silly. Blush

BOBBY UNDERWOOD GOT UP LATE AND FIXED himself a bowl of stale corn flakes and a cup of black coffee while he monitored his radios. He caught a little cross talk this morning from a rookie cop on patrol on the southside of Central Park. He only caught the end of the chatter about a black-haired girl leaving the Plaza Hotel. This was the best, and frankly, the only lead he had. He quickly showered and put on a rare, fresh pair of black jeans and an army-green T-shirt. As he showered, he started to think perhaps he was on to her. If the police noticed her, then something must have triggered the cop into looking at her. Something in his gut told him that he needed to get uptown and check out the lead.

He combed his oily black hair and brushed his teeth. He went into his bedroom and picked up his army jacket, and after a brief second, he opened the top drawer of his nightstand and pulled out the Luger. He held it in his hand for a second, then quickly stuffed it into the inside pocket of his jacket.

He went back to the kitchenette and opened an old, beat-up cookie jar. The jar was plain white with a painted chocolate cookie on the front. Inside was a small roll of twenty-dollar bills. This was Bobby's rainy-day fund. Alongside the cash was a black folding wallet with a genuine New York police badge and ID. He had gotten the forged credentials from a man in Brooklyn that specialized in such things. He stuffed it into the inside of his jacket next to the gun and quickly walked out the door to the subway station and then to the Plaza Hotel.

As Bobby was gearing up for his hunt, Colly and Josi were walking up Madison Avenue, window-shopping. They had gotten a late start after sleeping in at the hotel and fussing around, watching TV and chatting.

"Do you need to go home and get anything to take with you?" Colly asked Josi.

"No," Josi said after a brief minute of thought. "Definitely, no."

They had just eaten brunch at the hotel, which had turned out to be comical on a thousand levels. Colly *thought* she knew a lot about Earth manners and etiquette. Josi quickly found out that she did not. The final straw was when Colly sneezed into her mimosa and the orange liquid sprayed all over the table. Josi suspected Colly might be a little tipsy, but she wasn't sure. They talked about Josi and her job, her love of baseball, and boys. They laughed, and they cried.

Colly looked at her as they walked out onto the street. "Tell me more about this baseballs sport you mentioned that you like so much."

Josi laughed. "I will miss base*ball*, that's for sure."

Colly grabbed her by the wrist, and they stopped.

"Josi, you aren't going to miss anything. You ... we have the Blush, sweetheart. Gliese is an amazing place that holds a great many secrets and surprises."

"The Blush," Josi said. She raised her eyebrows and smiled.

"Yes," Colly went on as the girls walked arm in arm up Madison Avenue. "It's hard to explain, but all the things that you hold close to your heart, all the wonderfulness in your life, it's all there. You can visit many things if you focus. Don't worry, sweet sister, your Yonkees will still be there with you."

Josi laughed. "It's *Yankees*, silly."

"Yankees, Yonkees. Whatever you call them," Colly said nonchalantly and waved her hand.

The pair walked up the avenue, chatting and occasionally dipping into a boutique to look around. Colly seemed constantly entertained at the littlest things she saw. On the corner of Madison and Fifty-Second Street, Colly's eye caught an upscale adult toy store. She sidestepped quickly and made a beeline for the door. Her eyes bulged with curiosity.

"Easy, girl," Josi said as she giggled and pulled Colly by the arm back onto Madison.

Of course, Josi had to explain everything to her in great detail. She really didn't mind, as she knew Colly would return the favor when they got home to Gliese. They did make one purchase that morning. Josi bought them matching pink Yankees baseball caps. Colly loved hers and immediately put it on backward.

The girls slowly made their way up to the spot where they would get a car and head to the pickup zone. Neither sister would come out and say it, but they each had a pit in their stomach from the obvious statistic staring them in the face. Five percent.

Bad Bobby stood on the corner of Fifth Avenue and Fifty-Eighth Street and looked around nervously. Finally, he pulled his shoulders back and walked with fake bravado to the valet in front of the hotel. He whipped out his fake badge and flashed it to the young Puerto Rican kid.

"I'm looking for a girl that might be staying here. Black hair, very tall—"

That was all he needed to say. The kid's face lit up.

"*Si. Si.* Very pretty. With her twin, her twin. With a girl. White hair. *Muy llamativa!*"

Bobby tried to keep his composure and act like a cop. As soon as he said she was with her twin, that seemed to spark something inside of him that solidified Colly was the alien bitch he was looking for.

"Okay, have you seen them today?" Bobby asked as he tried to look and act the part of a cop.

"*Si!*" The kid pointed toward Madison Avenue.

Bobby smiled and thanked him. He trotted over to Madison Avenue and looked both ways. "Fuck," he growled, not knowing which way he should go.

Bobby didn't notice the real police officer across the street watching him closely. As soon as Bobby trotted away, the legitimate cop went up to the valet and had a quick chat with him. After a second or so, the rookie policeman started to trail Bad Bobby.

On Madison, Bobby looked across the street and saw a newspaper stand where a fat, older man smoked a cigar as he worked behind the counter. This time, a more confident Bobby strode right up to him and whipped out the badge; he felt like a badass version of Frank Serpico.

"Looking for two girls. Tall. One has black hair, the other white. You seen them?"

The cigar-smoking man nodded and puffed away.

"They bought two packs of cherry bubble gum and a couple of Milky Way bars. Paid me with a fifty and didn't want change. Real sweethearts. They went that way," he said and pointed up the street.

"How long ago?" Bobby asked, feeling giddy.

He shrugged. "Ten minutes, maybe?"

Bobby jogged up Madison Avenue, hot on their trail. Every block or so, he would flash his fictitious badge and ask pedestrians if they had seen the women. As luck would have it for Bad Bobby, everyone he asked had noticed the girls. They all shook their heads and pointed up the street in the direction the girls were headed. He was getting close. He could smell their cunts.

It was Josi who first noticed something was wrong.

"Colly, it's The Bump," she said and stopped in her tracks. She felt light-headed and scared.

Colly turned to her. "Wait … what?"

This time, it was Josi who had to tell Colly to focus.

"Focus, Colly. Can you feel it? Can you?"

Josi was starting to panic ever so slightly. She looked back and forth and pulled Colly into a little alley right off Madison. She pushed Colly down on a trash can; she put her forehead against her sister's and whispered, "Colly, something wants to hurt us."

Colly looked around, feeling unsure. "Come on, Josi, let's boogie. We need to go now."

They peeked out from the alley, looked back and forth, and started moving a little faster. The original quick plan was to skirt the park until the crowds thinned out a little, take a car, and start heading back to the pickup spot. Hopefully, they would be there right after dark. As far as the sisters could tell, nobody knew about their plans. How could they? Colly assumed the government was well aware that she was on Earth and probably had figured out she was in New York, but she was sure they didn't know why she was here, and she hoped they didn't know anything about Josi. She was confident that by the time they got a handle on things, they would be home on Gliese.

As soon as they made it a few blocks, they turned and ducked into the park. Josi, who was almost in tears at this point, whimpered and clung to her sister. Together, they pushed through a small row of shrubs and onto a rarely used dirt path that only the park's maintenance workers used as a cut-through. Occasionally, joggers also used the path to avoid the crowds and traffic. This afforded the girls some quick privacy in order to catch their breath and get a plan together.

"Who is it? Talk to me, Josi," Colly said sternly.

The girls again put their foreheads together and held hands.

"Josi! Stop shaking!" Colly ordered as their foreheads rested against each other's. Josi was about to say something, but they both froze at the sound of a gun's hammer cocking close to their ears.

18

Stick 'Em Up. Black Blood. R8

BOBBY HELD THE LUGER JUST INCHES FROM Colly's head and smiled nervously. He was a full eight inches shorter than the sisters, so he looked up and the gun was at an angle pointed toward the sky.

"My first alien-bitch hunt." Bobby snickered as his bravado spiked and bubbled. His adrenaline pumped full force as he looked at the girls. In a quick flash of adolescent immaturity, Bobby wondered if it would be possible to fuck them both at the same time.

"Here's what's going to happen, ladies," Bobby said, practically salivating. He knew the girls would be lookers, but he, like a lot of other people, wasn't prepared for exactly how odd and alluring they would be.

"Let's all three of us very nicely take a little walk back to my place. Any fucked-up funny shit and at least one of you cunts is going to get shot in the heart. No tricks, no sudden moves. All smiles and everyone lives."

Josi snapped her jaw and leaned slightly toward Bobby in a primal Gliesen gesture that she had no idea was tucked into her Star Child DNA. Her lower jaw pushed forward, and she could feel a slight tingle in her lower back that spread down her crotch and into her legs. "Who are you?" she asked in a deep voice.

He ignored her as he allowed his sexual fantasies run wild in his head. He was going to rape them. Maybe make them watch each other. It was going to be a fine night.

He was just about to say something when a teenage girl who was volunteering in the park turned the corner and froze. She gasped, dropped the tray of azaleas she was carrying, and quickly ran the other way.

In that very instant, Colly glared at Bobby, inhaled a huge gulp of air, and held it. In her head, she saw that he raped and abused women. She watched as he beat a girl unconscious with an old lava lamp, raped her, and ejaculated into her mouth while she lay on the floor of her apartment comatose from being hit so many times. She saw him beating a black-and-white alley cat with a rusty pipe until it died yowling, in miserable pain. She saw him insert an M-80 firecracker into a puppy's mouth and laugh hysterically as the baby yellow lab ran around with its lower jaw disintegrated. Colly's eyes began to squint ever so slightly as she watched Bad Bobby.

"Fuck! Fuck!" Bobby said as he turned to see the young girl racing out of the park and looking around for help.

Just as Colly was about to pounce on Bobby and release her incomprehensible rage on him, Josi shot her hand out and clamped onto Bobby's sweat-stained neck. Her hand hit him so fast and with such ferocity that he had no time to even flinch. Bobby let out a comically feminine shriek as the German Luger slipped out of his hand and hit the dirt trail with an undramatic, metallic thump. He grabbed Josi's wrist and tried to twist it loose, to no avail.

His eyes bulged and he muttered and gasped, "You fuckin' cun—" Then he could speak no more. Josi was remembering the girl Tabatha in the dirty alley and how this motherfucker had shoved a beer bottle into her vagina and kicked it in.

Colly watched, expressionless, as Josi began to dig her fingers into his neck. In a strange mirror-like imitation of her sister, her jaw pushed forward while her shoulders rolled back. She could hear Josi crushing the small bones and tendons of his spine and neck. It sounded like someone was cracking dried fishbones on a log. Her index finger eventually punctured the skin and slipped into his flesh right up to the second knuckle. Blood flowed around Josi's wrist and poured down Bobby's chest. Bobby gurgled and instantly fell to the ground like a sack of garbage. Days later, when the coroner was performing Bobby's autopsy, he would note into his tape recorder that the assailant's hand hit his throat with such force that two of his molars were broken in half and another two were cracked.

Only Josi and Colly could see that the blood on the ground and on Josi's hand was jet black. Ink black, like gooey tar on a hot city street. To everyone else, the blood was normal, red and sticky. Not to the Geminis, though. The two were able to confirm what they, and a great many other people, had suspected. Bobby had a rotten and decaying soul. A Black Blood. Like bad meat that was left in the sun. An evil man of the human species. There was no doubt to the sisters that despite earthly law, Earth was better off with Bobby gone. Much better off.

They stood over Bobby's disgusting corpse while the sounds of the city continued uninterrupted. Somewhere in the distance, children laughed, and car horns continued to blare. The sisters looked at each other and simultaneously raised their eyebrows.

"Are you okay?" Josi asked Colly.

Colly looked around quickly.

"Yeah. Yeah, I'm okay. Are you?"

Josi shrugged.

"Yeah, I'm good. Am I going to—"

"Don't fucking move!"

Josi and Colly jumped as three police officers walked toward them from the west side of the park. The three huge officers with their guns drawn moved closer to the girls; their eyes danced between Bobby's body and the sisters. The lead policeman was the rookie cop that had been following Bobby and Colly.

"Let me see your hands!" the lead officer barked as one of the other officers called for backup on his handheld radio.

Colly and Josi froze. Josi let out a gasp, and her mouth stayed open. A sharp twinge in Colly's ear caused her to tilt her head slightly, and then, in her head, she heard Josi's voice.

Run, Colly! Run!

Both girls exploded in an instant and were off running across the Great Lawn.

"Stop!" the officer yelled and gave chase.

Colly and Josi sprinted in gazelle-like strides across the Great Lawn. They easily outpaced and outran the out-of-shape NYPD officers. As they sprinted across the baseball fields, the players all stopped and stared in disbelief as the strange-looking set of twins in pink Yankees ball caps covered the infield of the diamond in four or five easy strides. Just as the girls were midway across the infield, the hitter slashed a line drive up the middle. Josi effortlessly leaped over the spinning ball.

The shortstop from the home team nodded in approval and said to the second baseman, "Do you think we can get them to play softball for us?"

Both girls knew they could comfortably outrun the police who were giving chase, but they knew they couldn't outrun the radios they were carrying.

As they ran across the Winterdale Arch, it was Colly who noticed several officers running toward them from the Ross Playground.

"Josi, right!" Colly screamed.

Both girls broke right in unison and dashed north, then west, and finally out of the park and onto West Eighty-Third Street.

They blended into the crowd as much as they could, but they knew that wouldn't last long with the two of them breathing heavily and Josi's hand covered in drying blood. All those police officers would track them sooner rather than later.

Within a minute, the sound of sirens closing in began to fill the street between the buildings. The high-pitched wails began bouncing around the block, and Josi began to feel dizzy and sick. Her crotch felt numb and her feet tingled. She grabbed Colly's arm and went down on one knee.

"Josi!" Colly screamed as she held her. "Josi, get up! C'mon, Josi! Up!"

She looked around at the gathering crowd while the sirens got louder. Several people laughed while they took pictures and videos.

Josi's face was frozen in a scream. She thrust her hands up to her ears and suddenly, every window on the block exploded in a violent, booming detonation. The only sound you could hear for the next few seconds was the sound of glass raining down on the street. Car alarms blared and the crowd screamed and covered their heads with their hands. Colly ducked and smiled at her sister's antics.

Later that night, the local news quoted a FEMA spokesman, who said the windows broke as a result of what he called a centralized microquake.

"Let's go, Josi! Now!" she yelled in her sister's face.

Josi seemed to snap back to reality in an instant, and she grabbed Colly's hand and darted around the corner.

"We need a car!" she yelled to Colly as they ran down the street block by block.

"This one! This one!" Colly said and pointed frantically at a new, black Audi R8 with the sticker still in the window across Eighty-Eighth Street.

"What! No, Colly. We'll stick out like a sore thumb. Let's grab that one." She pointed to a rather ordinary Honda SUV.

Colly smiled and continued pointing frantically at the Audi.

"Oh, for fuck's sake, fine," Josi said and rolled her eyes and grinned slightly.

The girls ran across the street hand in hand to the R8 that was parked directly in front of the Audi of Manhattan dealership. The car was as clean as a new pin and awaiting its new owner. The sticker in the window had a price of $208,000. Colly tried the door. Locked. Josi looked over her shoulder at the group of salesmen looking out the huge front window of the showroom, jabbering and pointing frantically at them.

"Hurry up!" she barked at Colly.

Colly found the center of the door handle with the tip of her index finger and slowly glided her finger back and forth. Both doors clicked open instantly.

They jumped in and slammed the doors just as the group of overweight, middle-aged salesmen ran out the front door.

"Go, Colly! Go!" Josi yelled as she looked out the small back window at the angry pack of salesmen quickly closing in on them.

She extended her index finger and touched the center of the steering wheel gently, and the R8 roared to life. Colly mashed the gas pedal and they were off like a rocket down Eighty-Eighth Street, heading to the West Side Highway and then north to the pickup zone.

Less than fifteen minutes later, the Audi dealership was crawling with local New York police and a dozen feds. The feds all seemed to be looking around out on the street, while the locals were inside the dealership. The employees could only describe the car thieves as two women, very tall, one with jet-black hair and the other with stark-white hair.

The sales manager was upset at the loss of a brand-new, just-purchased R8, but even he thought the presence of hundreds of local police and the slew of federal agents outside seemed like a slight case of overkill. No one bothered to fill the overweight, coffee-swilling manager in on the fact that the two girls were actually alien life forces that had landed on the planet and had just choked the life out of a man right off Madison Avenue.

On the lighter side, they also didn't mention to him that one of them had destroyed six F-22 fighters and more than a dozen F-16s; somehow deactivated a top-secret surface-to-air missile that cost roughly $65 million and was now at the bottom of the Atlantic; crashed a Jaguar F-type into a hair salon on Fifty-Fourth Street; and had been causing panic among governments all over the world. He also didn't mention that for some bizarre reason, they had reverse engineered every electronic device in their suite at the Plaza Hotel. Or how they caused some kind of commotion at the firehouse on Fifty-First Street, and now, they had just stolen an Audi R8.

19

Hawkeye at 20,000.
Echo One, Echo One

GENERAL WALLIS PACED IN HIS OFFICE AT THE Cheyenne complex in Wyoming. He hadn't slept much over the last couple days, and he had been on the phone with the president every few hours, giving him top-secret updates. In his hand was a glossy 8x10 photograph that had been delivered to him earlier that day. He kept glancing down at it.

They had found the craft shortly after it landed. It was dumb luck that a hunter stumbled on it so quickly and called the sheriff, who called the state police. Now their little visitor had killed a man in Central Park and had apparently stolen another fine sports car practically from under the noses of the NYPD.

The craft was packed up and rushed to Dayton Air Force Base temporarily before making its way to Area 51 in Nevada. It revealed very little information they could use right now, and frankly, the technicians and scientists were pessimistic about any future use. It seemed as though most of the controls and what appeared to be a navigation system had been destroyed. As interesting and complex as the remains were, there would clearly be no way to reverse engineer the components.

General Wallis sat down at his desk and rubbed the bridge of his nose. He looked at the photo again—one of the hundreds of times he did so that day. The photo showed the inside of the craft's cockpit. Written above the burned-out control in a blackish-blue ink was the message, "Have fun, Space Girl! Say hi to Buddy Presley for me!"

Obviously, this was some type of complex code in disguise. According to the techs in Dayton, it was perhaps a trigger code for an invasion. They also theorized it might be a message to other alien life forms already on the planet. Either way, the simple and confusing message was most troubling.

He had heard back from Galaxy Control, and they confirmed that no extraterrestrials were scheduled to be anywhere near Earth for at least six months. At that point, a single ship was due to land in the Sahara Desert to take air samples for an intergalactic study. If this was true, that meant that the alien was an unauthorized visitor. That could mean trouble.

The red phone on his desk rang. The general picked it up on the first ring.

"General Wallis," he answered.

"General Wallis, this is command. We've got them," the colonel on the other end of the line stated with reserved excitement.

"Where? And what do you mean, 'them?'" the general asked as he stood up behind his huge oak desk. He continued to stare down at the 8x10 glossy picture.

"Them, sir. We have two of them in a vehicle heading north out of New York on the Henry Hudson Parkway. Both are female. Sir, they appear to be twins, or at least sisters. They match the description from our people on the ground in New York. We're starting to piece together what happened over the last couple hours or so. We interviewed the teenage volunteer in the park and the people who saw them take the car. Hell, a hundred people saw them being chased by the NYPD, and most got a good look at them."

"Do not engage, Colonel. Let's let out the line a little and see where they take us. Who's watching them?"

"We have a Hawkeye in the sky at twenty-thousand feet. They don't know he's up there."

"Good. Keep me posted, and Colonel … give them a little room. I want to see how this shakes out. Let's give them thirty minutes and see what happens."

"Copy that, General. We have plenty of manpower here if we need it," the colonel said and hung up.

The general looked at the photo for another quick second and then pushed the intercom to ring for his secretary.

"Yes, General," his assistant said in a nondescript voice.

"Get me the secretary of defense on the line. If he's sleeping, wake his ass up."

The twins had been rocketing north toward the pickup zone in the R8 for about twenty minutes. At some point, Josi got concerned that no one was actually chasing them. She knew there was no way they could get away that easily. A thousand people had seen them tear out of the dealership with the R8 and turn north. Surely, they had to have roadblocks and helicopters, like they did in the movies.

"Ummmm ... Colly, how come nobody is chasing us?" Josi said calmly and let out a little laugh.

Colly shrugged and let off the gas. She slowed down to a more acceptable speed, looked over her shoulder, and slid into the right-hand lane. "They know where we are."

"How? How do you know that?" Josi asked and grabbed Colly's arm. "And take off those stupid goggles! You don't need them to drive!"

Colly made a pouty face and pushed the goggles up on her head.

Josi repeated herself. "How do you know that they know where we are?"

"There's an airplane up there watching us. Focus, Josi, and you'll see it. It's called an Eye Hawk, or something like that. It doesn't really matter. Hopefully, we'll be gone before they can get their shit together and catch us."

Josi closed her eyes, focused, breathed deep—and nothing happened.

"I can't see it," she said matter-of-factly. She leaned over and grabbed the goggles off Colly's head.

"Where did you get these? They look old."

"That guy, Fietch, I was telling you about. The smuggler that arranged this gave them to me. I have no idea where or how he got them."

"How much farther?" Josi asked and slipped on the goggles. "What do you think?" she said and grinned at Colly.

"I love them, and not too far, I think," she replied and laughed at her sister.

Just then, a helicopter swooped down low and buzzed the R8. The Blackhawk turned right and quickly disappeared behind the trees.

"Fuck!" Josi screamed as the R8 swerved.

"You didn't see *that* coming!" Josi screamed again.

Colly bit her lip and gripped the steering wheel tightly. The R8 surged forward as the turbos whined and the machine blasted down the highway. Colly was following an internal instinct that was gently pushing her to the pickup spot.

Inside the Blackhawk chopper, the pilot radioed the patrol cars that were positioned up the highway waiting to pounce on the R8.

"Echo one, Echo one, this is Skyhawk. Target, one zero miles out."

Colly looked at Josi quickly.

"Josi, focus on that helicopter thingy. Focus and put it down."

Josi immediately obeyed her sister and closed her eyes so all she could hear was the sound of the car's motor smashing through the higher RPMs. She held her breath and let it out slowly.

Nine hundred feet above them, the Blackhawk's motor began to slowly lose power.

"Mayday! Mayday! Mayday!" the pilot called out frantically while trying in vain to get a restart on the engine.

The chopper drifted and sputtered as it lost altitude steadily. The experienced pilot struggled as he tried to control the Blackhawk. It skidded across a playground and landed hard in the middle of a high school parking lot five miles away.

"Good job, Josi! Now, there are police cars ahead. Focus, Sis. Take 'em down."

She closed her eyes and went through the steps again. She saw a line of police cars idling ahead with their parking lights on. Five miles up the road, all the engines seized in the state patrol cars, and their batteries started leaking and bubbling acid everywhere. The confused troopers all started turning the keys, looking around frantically. The cars' engines turned over sluggishly but would not start.

"Woo-hoo!" Colly screamed, and Josi laughed. She still wore the vintage goggles.

Colly whipped the car onto the off-ramp and sped down a country road, turbos spinning out. A deer leaped across the road in a big, single bound five hundred feet in front of them.

"What in the holy fuck is that?" Colly yelled.

"That's a deer, sweetheart," Josi said and giggled.

The pair burned up the country road for a mile or so, when Josi started fidgeting in her seat.

"More are coming, Colly! Lots more!" Josi said as she looked out the back window.

"It's too late for them! We're here!" Colly slowed down the R8.

The car whipped off the side of the road and skidded to a rough stop close to an abandoned picnic area. The doors flew open, and the sisters jumped out and ran toward the woods, with Colly leading the way. They both tried to find a trail or path, to no avail. They pushed blindly forward into the darkening woods, unsure and afraid, as they knew their fate would be decided very soon. In a very short time, they hoped to see the orb sitting idle in the woods, waiting to return to Gliese. They prayed to the same God as they dashed into the woods.

20

Where's the Orb? Stuck on Earth. The Great Water Plains

THE COOL WIND BLEW THEIR HAIR STEADILY across their faces in wisps as a pack of coyotes howled and whined in the distance. Colly led the pair quickly through the night, guided by witch light and moonlight. At one point, both girls fell face forward at the same time and landed flat on their chests with a grunt.

"Fuck!" Josi said as they helped each other up.

"My hat!" Colly yelled. She picked up her Yankees cap and put it back on her head, backward.

They could hear sirens in the distance and the *chop, chop, chop* of military helicopters from somewhere far away. The sounds of voices calling out to each other were closing in on them.

Colly looked up through the treetops toward the heavens with a deep look of focus on her face and repeated, "Please, please, please …"

"Colly!" Josi screamed as she looked back into the woods where the voices were coming from. "They're coming! The police are coming!"

The orb was nowhere to be seen. Colly fell to her knees and started to cry. "Oh, no!" she wailed.

"Now what?" Josi fell on her knees next to Colly. She dropped her head on Colly's shoulder.

"We run! We have to get back to New York and figure this out. Oh my God, Josi! We're stuck here!" Colly said, hysterical.

They both looked over their shoulders toward the voices. The feds were closing in.

"Okay! Up, sweetheart. Let's move!" Josi pulled Colly to her feet.

The pair stood up; they held onto one another and cried. Just then, the wind stopped, and the coyotes' howls ceased. The girls froze and looked at each other. A timber rattlesnake, inches from Colly's feet, attempted to bury itself deeper under a mossy rock moss in panic. The air turned static and tasted like copper.

The light approached them from behind. As they turned to face it, the hair on Josi's arms stood up. Her bladder felt full, and her breathing became choppy and harsh. Despite her best efforts, she was afraid.

The light draped around the ancient tree stumps and greasy, moss-covered rocks as it approached. It wasn't universal light, but a new type of light that seemed to be liquid. It flowed and dripped like thin lava as it inched forward.

Josi reached out and fumbled awkwardly for Colly's hand. Colly squeezed it reassuringly.

"Don't be afraid," she whispered to Josi as the light engulfed them in a push of warm air. The trees in the forest seemed to spread apart all at once and bend inward as if they were bowing to the strange light, like a god. A whoosh of warm air pushed through the woods, and a craft appeared.

"Oh. My. Fuck," Colly said, wide-eyed, and smiled. The craft settled on the forest floor, and in an instant, the side panel slid open and a familiar and vague shape appeared.

"Space Girl!" the figure bellowed and laughed. It was the dirty pirate, Fietch.

"Fietch?" Colly said, shocked.

"Ha ha ha ha! Did you think I was going to let you stay here?" Fietch replied and smiled. "C'mon, Space Girls!"

He held out his meaty hand and helped Josi and Colly into the craft. Colly looked up front and saw Fietch's henchman, Books, at the controls, watching the girls climb aboard. He shot Colly a cold sneer and turned back around.

"Fietch! I ... I can't believe it! Fietch!"

Colly hugged the fat pirate and pointed to Josi.

"This is my sister. This is Josi."

"Welcome aboard, Earth Girl!" Fietch hugged Josi and laughed.

"Hold on, everyone." Books snarled.

The craft rose slightly and hovered for a moment, and then a flash of light lit up the area and the craft was gone.

Seconds later, the forest was quiet and still. The timber rattlesnake peeked out from under its mossy rock, looked around, coiled back up, and went to sleep. The air returned to normal, and somewhere in the distance, the coyotes began to howl again. The pack of federal agents stopped in their tracks and looked around and up.

As a last little quip from the sisters, the feds all felt their bladders let loose at once, wetting the front of their khaki pants. Josi and Colly laughed as they stared out the port window. Josi stuck up her middle finger. Even Books, the ruthless button man, let out a little laugh. Then, in a flash, they were gone.

Ten thousand Earth years were condensed into a single blink of the eye as space and time folded and twisted in odd and seemingly unimaginable shapes. The fabric of time and existence fell upon itself as the craft with its precious cargo bolted instantly through its wormholes.

The craft burst back into the Gliesen atmosphere with a flash of blue light. The ship hooked a hard right out of space, and Books quickly got the craft under control. Fietch had told Books to drop the craft at the base of the Great Water Plains. Twenty minutes later, they were on the ground.

The Geminis gingerly stepped out of the ship, hand in hand. Colly spoke in a strange tongue that somehow, Josi could easily understand.

"We're home, Star Child," she said and smiled excitedly at Josi.

Colly's enchanting world of cyan blues and kyanite greens sparkled under a lavish cerulean sky streaked with umber, punctuated only by the six Gliesen moons.

Josi's mouth dropped in astonishment, and she began to cry.

"Thank you, Gemini. I'm finally home."

Epilogue: Book 1

General Wallis sat at his desk in Cheyenne and read the final report from the Shooting Star team. The general shook his head and smiled. He stood up, lit a cigarette, and walked over to the big window that overlooked the main control room inside the mammoth bunker. He took a long drag and puffed smoke rings, which the indoor ventilation system instantly took care of.

The report was generally complete and detailed what had happened in the short forty-eight hours or so that the Gliesen girl was on Earth. She had killed a man in cold blood in Central Park, and that was extremely unfortunate. It was quickly learned through DNA samples that the man who was murdered, Robert Underwood, was responsible for a slew of brutal rapes around lower Manhattan. Attached to the report in a separate folder were all the NYPD's reports on the unsolved rapes. Wallis read through them briefly and shook his head in disgust at the details.

The report was inconclusive as to the reason the extraterrestrial had come to Earth. Inquiries were made at Galaxy Control, but they proved to be fruitless. None of the Galactic representatives were aware of her, or so they said.

The only thing Wallis knew for sure was she came by herself but left with another. He leafed through the stacks of photographs that had been taken by civilians and stopped at a picture of the two girls that a security camera had snapped close to the car dealership. He stared at it for a long time. The picture showed the two women looking directly into the camera with desperation etched deep on their faces. The general pulled this pic out and set it to the side. Later, he pinned it to his cluttered bulletin board. From time to time, he would look at the picture and wonder what was going through their heads at that exact moment.

Wallis finished his cigarette, picked up the file, and placed it in a large sealed and tamper-proof envelope that simply read: "Top Secret—Star Child. SETI/NORAD Eyes Only." That envelope was put into a briefcase that he took with him to the SETI outpost in Nevada, where it was placed in a large, secure filing cabinet along with hundreds of other top-secret folders.

BOOK TWO

1

Home Sweet Home.
Top Secret Twins. Peek-a-Boo

DAWN WAS JUST BEGINNING TO BREAK ON Gliese. Early-morning fog swirled along the beach as the warm wind blew gently and steadily along the shoreline. The rich smell of salty air pulled inland by the solar wind engulfed everything it touched.

Colly and Josi jogged along the surf with their steady footfalls in perfect rhythm as the waves crashed and the surf boomed. Both girls turned sharply toward the sea just as the sun broke the clouds, revealing the brilliant blue sky laced with streaks of painted red and green clouds.

"Pretty," Josi remarked with her arms pumping smoothly.

Colly nodded. "Uh-huh. Pretty, pretty."

The sisters were on the last mile of their five-mile daily run along Alulla Beach in the North Vega Territory of Gliese. This had been Colly's home her entire life and for the last two years was Josi's home, too.

The run was part of their daily routine. The sisters were both in amazing shape, and aside from the daily run, they both took yoga three times a week, cycled whenever they could find time, and they both had become experts on self-defense and martial arts.

In the two years after coming home to Gliese, Josi had settled in comfortably and was now a teacher in the territory school system. She taught Earth studies, which was an advanced class for exceptionally bright pupils. Of course, Colly continued her career in engineering and was now head of project development at her firm. Both of the girls loved and excelled at their jobs.

They lived less than two blocks from each other and spent nearly every day together. Most of the time, they would sit on Colly's balcony, which overlooked the ocean, and sip coffee while dishing about work, current events, and their social lives. Colly had helped Josi adapt and adjust to her new life on Gliese, and they were both pleasantly surprised at how quickly Josi was able to assimilate to Gliesen culture and tradition. Of course, Josi always seemed to have questions about culture and history, and she spent a great deal of her free time in the public library and on her computer, studying. Luckily for Josi, Colly was a patient and accommodating tutor.

Two years earlier, there had been questions to be answered after they returned home from Earth. The Council of Generalship did indeed summon them to appear before the court shortly after their return to Gliese, which was not unexpected. The girls sat stony-faced in front of the council while they were asked questions and inquiries were made. Both were given legal advisors before the hearing, and both were advised that they would probably be looking at spending some time in the House of Detention. Upon hearing this, Josi and Colly looked at each other from across the table with troubled expressions, while their worry lines cut through their otherwise insouciant posture.

Surprisingly, the hearing was relatively quick, and both Colly and Josi were honest and forthcoming in answering the questions. Neither sister dropped her eyes or showed any sign of weakness. Underneath the large wooden table, the sisters held hands. In the end, the council closed the case, and the girls were told that they were free to go. Both the girls' advisors looked at each other and clandestinely shrugged.

Fifteen minutes after the court had dismissed, the generalship had retired to a lavish back conference room. All nine of the members loosened their robes and sat at the table in an uncharacteristically casual manner.

"They have no idea, do they?" Pancros, the council's most senior member, asked the room while pouring himself a glass of water from the pitcher in the middle of the table.

The rest of the council sat quietly in relaxed thought. Finally, Rigel, who had a reputation as a bit of a fundamentalist among the council, spoke quietly but firmly. "I think Colly does."

"At this point, it really doesn't matter," Pancros said and continued. "Rigel, if Colly knows, doesn't it stand to reason Josi does, too?"

"Hard to say with any degree of certainty," Rigel said. "Let's assume she does. Until we need them, does it really matter?"

"No. Probably not," Pancros said with finality.

Pancros stood up and put his hands on the table to address the council as a group.

"The day will come when we need them. Until such a time, I think it's a good idea to keep an eye on them. I think they will be preoccupied for quite some time getting Josi adapted to Gliese, but a year from now, two? Three years, maybe? Who knows what they will discover, if anything. In some ways, the less they know, the better. Sooner or later, they may put the pieces together and understand they are the last of a lethal and dying breed. Until that time, we just sit tight."

The council members nodded almost in unison and agreed to watch and wait in regard to the twins. For now, the status quo would remain.

As the council broke up and prepared to leave on summer recess, Rigel and Pancros stood by themselves in the corner and looked out the window at the cityscape. Its mammoth buildings rose into the sky as far as you could see. They spoke in lowered voices, deliberately out of earshot from the rest.

"You knew the mother?" Rigel asked as he lit a cigarette.

"Calista? Yes. Very well," Pancros replied, with a touch of nostalgia in his voice.

"She died on Earth, from what I've read. Is that right? Or maybe someplace close?" Rigel took a long drag off his cigarette.

"She died on Earth. The twins were very young—newborns, actually. She had them on Earth with the intent to bring them home to Gliese. Things got … complicated there. Calista was killed, and the American Earth government was in a bad spot. They found the twins, and, well … let's just say through a series of … miscommunications, Josi was placed in an earthly home, while we made arrangements for Colly to come back here, to Gliese." Pancros sighed and pushed on. "It wasn't ideal, and we were under pressure from both systems, Earth and Gliese, to wrap the situation up quickly and quietly. I knew eventually Colly would want to get her sister. Frankly, I thought it might have been sooner."

Rigel listened intently and said, "You were the one who pushed us to deny her access to Earth, Pancros."

"So I did," he replied with sigh. "So now we have both of them here." Pancros lowered his voice as he spoke. "They are the last of the breed. They are the last Star Hunters, and once they are gone, that race will be extinct."

Rigel nodded and said quietly, "They are lethal, Pancros."

Pancros sighed. "I know, old friend, but they are the last."

After finishing their run, the girls toweled off and settled into comfy chairs that overlooked the massive Sea of Tranquility. The sky was a brilliant blue, and the day meteors streaked through the sky almost nonstop.

Josi gazed out over the constant surf and felt physically content in her new world. It was as if her old life was a simple waypoint on her journey to a more permanent existence. Like every booming wave that crashed into the sand eroding grain after grain after grain, she felt her past life was washing away like the grains of sand. This was her home, not Earth. She was indeed Gliese, through and through.

After a minute of silence, Colly turned her head and read her sister's nostalgic thoughts.

"Do you miss it? Earth, your life there?" Colly asked and looked back out into the blue sky.

"No, I don't, and please stop reading me! I don't peekaboo into you," Josi said angrily.

"You don't miss going to the Yankees Stadium?" Colly ribbed her, ignoring her last statement.

"It's Yank*ee* Stadium, silly," Josi said.

"Well, do you miss it?" Colly prodded.

"I do, but I don't, Colly. It's hard to explain." Josi stood up and stretched.

Colly got the feeling she was dancing around the topic a little.

"I'm going home. I have to shower and go to work, don't you?"

Colly shook her head. "No, I'm working from home today. I have to go to the market later. Can I grab you anything while I'm there?"

"Ummm ... yeah," Josi said as she pulled the strings tight on her day bag. "Can you grab me dark chocolate and powdered sugar?"

Colly nodded and smiled at Josi as she started out the door headed to her house.

"And stay out of my head, Colly!" Josi scolded her sister as she was about to close the front door. "I'm kinda horny, and unless you feel like being traumatized, stay out!"

Colly covered her mouth and giggled. Josi slammed the door deliberately harder than she had to.

As soon as Josi left, Colly grabbed a glass of iced tea, walked back out onto the balcony, and looked out over the sea. She sighed and narrowed her eyes. Something was coming. She didn't know what, but something was coming. She could see that Josi knew it too, but perhaps, like herself, she was afraid of what it might be.

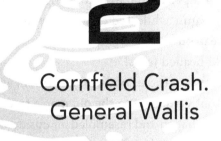

2

Cornfield Crash.
General Wallis

IN THE SCORCHING-HOT NEVADA SUN, AT AN undisclosed location north of Las Vegas, General Wallis watched as a pair of T-38 chase planes flew low and slow over the makeshift command center. The facility was, in actuality, just a few air-conditioned mobile homes full of electronic equipment and monitoring devices. A few seconds later, an alien craft followed, arching across the sky as it gained speed and altitude at a mesmerizing rate.

"Impressive," Wallis said to himself as he looked through his binoculars. "Damn impressive."

The craft, code named Phoenix, was a recovered vehicle from two years ago that had crashed near the city of Youngstown, Ohio. Just after midnight, a farmer and his wife in the suburb of Canfield heard an incredibly loud screeching noise as the craft burst through their cornfield and skidded across the driveway to end up on its side in the front lawn. Most of the freshly planted rose bushes were destroyed, along with a garden gnome that ended up being launched seventy-five feet into a potato patch. The farmer, Teddy Burnett, and his wife, Jody, were thrown out of their bed onto the floor.

"The shit was that?" Jody asked sleepily but wide-eyed.

"How the hell should I know?" Teddy screamed. "Did a car hit the house? Was that a bomb?"

Jody clambered over Ted and started crawling toward the window. Ted grabbed her ankle.

"Wait, wait, wait!" he said. "I'll look; go get my gun."

Jody obediently jumped up and went to a long cardboard box under the bed to retrieve the gun, while Ted crawled over to the window and slowly peeked his head out.

"Holy moly, bald-headed Jesus!"

Jody and Ted stared out the second-story bedroom window in utter disbelief. In their front yard, next to the old maple tree, was a craft of some sort. It was oval shaped and resembled an upside-down acorn; it looked like something out of a sci-fi movie.

"I think I wet my pajamas, Teddy!" Jody said in a harsh whisper as they continued to stare out the window, their moon faces slack-jawed and stunned.

The following morning, Ted and Jody sat in the back of the sheriff's station with several men from the FBI and SETI. They were the same men that showed up at the farm the night before and whisked them off to a local motel. As the agents explained it, a top-secret Air Force jet had lost an engine, and unfortunately, it had separated above the farm and landed on their property. Of course, this was a top-secret project that required patriots like the Burnetts to do their country a great service and keep the incident to themselves.

In front of the nervous couple was a stack of papers marked "Top Secret." Both Jody and Ted signed the confidentiality papers willingly enough, and the nice man from the government offered to buy the farm at a laughable and ridiculously high price, stating that there may be trace radiation on the property. Later that month, the farm was sold to The United States of America, and newly retired Ted and Jody were in Florida in a magnificently opulent condo on the beach, compliments of the US taxpayers.

General Wallis lowered his binoculars and stepped into the trailer. A blast of icy-cold air greeted him as he opened the door.

"Gentlemen," Wallis said, acknowledging the small group of young scientists from NASA.

"General, everything seems to be working other than the intergalactic cloak. I'll be damned if we can figure that one out." NASA's top scientist, an MIT grad, scratched his head almost comically as he spoke.

Just as Wallis started to say something, the phone on the wall began to buzz. The general excused himself and reached out to get the phone.

"Command, General Wallis here." The general closed his eyes as he spoke almost curtly to the voice on the other end of the line. "When? Are you sure? Are they still in New York? How do you know that, Lieutenant?"

He hung up quickly, waited a second, and then picked the receiver back up and said, "Get me a chopper out to satellite command ASAP."

Fifteen minutes later, he was on that chopper headed to Area 51 to catch the Janet flight to Vegas. From there, he took to an Air Force Learjet to Dulles and then grabbed a car that would take him to a secure meeting site.

3

Tiggy, Jake, and Arch. Bridge Lessons. The Bad Ones

BETWEEN THE BROOKLYN AND MANHATTAN bridges, along the boardwalk in the Dumbo neighborhood, the trio sat on one of the vintage-looking benches that overlooked the city.

"That particular bridge was built in Earth year 1869," Tiggy said with an air of boastful, knowledgeable pride, while she pointed at the mighty Brooklyn Bridge.

"I guess you know your earthen history, don't you?" Jake said, irritated, while he brushed Tiggy's blowing red hair out of his face.

"Now, that bridge ..." Tiggy continued with her spontaneous lesson on bridges. "That bridge is called the Manhattan Bridge, and it was built in Earth year 1901, but it wasn't finished for almost ten years."

"Nobody gives a fuck, Tig," Arch said quickly and a little loudly as he flipped his cigarette butt into the Hudson River, clearly irritated. "Save the earthly history lessons for someone who gives a shit."

"Fuck off," Tiggy said quietly, under her breath.

The three, Tiggy, Arch, and Jake, had been in New York for less than a week, and they were already becoming restless, bored, and worried. They spent their days much like this one, sitting on a bench and doing nothing.

Arch, the trio's unspoken leader, had taken care of getting them to Earth and hidden in one of the planet's largest metropolises. It wasn't easy, and he had a sickly suspicion that the Gliesen authorities knew where they were. He knew that the orb probably had a tracking device, and he doubted very strongly that that had gone overlooked. He assumed and hoped the Gliesen government would have to spend countless months and resources negotiating with the Earth authorities on a plan to come for them. He was counting on this, and who knew, perhaps it would not be worth the trouble to come find them.

As of this moment, they were intergalactic fugitives. All three thought that it had a nice ring to it: *intergalactic fugitives*. They were no longer just outlaws on Gliese, but intergalactic outlaws. Yep, they were badass.

Three weeks ago on Gliese, the group had, in partial desperation, started a string of high-end armed robberies. For the most part, they had gone off without a hitch, and that was a good thing. Then, on a warm and sticky night, the trio robbed a well-to-do home on the outskirts of town. Just as they were getting ready to leave, the homeowner opened the front door. Everyone froze in the dimly lit living room.

"Easy does it," the homeowner said calmly. "Let's all just relax."

Nobody moved; nobody spoke. You could have heard the proverbial pin drop. The homeowner slowly put down a bag of groceries and raised his hands.

"Arrrch ..." Tiggy said calmly.

Suddenly, the room exploded in a flash of light, and it felt like the world had just exploded. The homeowner, later identified as Major Cy Damen, spun around as most of the left side of his head disintegrated into a fine pink mist. The wall directly behind the major looked as if someone had instantly painted it red. Major Damen's body, less one half of a head, spun around and landed at the foot of the stairs with a *thump*.

At the time, the trio had no idea they had just ventilated the head of a major in the Gliesen Planetary Guard. That was obviously a huge problem for them. On Gliese, that was a capital crime, with no appeal after the verdict. If caught, they would be executed within a month. The swift hand of justice wasted no time when it came to capital-murder cases on Gliese.

"Shit! Shit!" Jake barked. "What the fuck?" His hands ran through his hair as he looked down at the twisted and bloody corpse.

Tiggy let out little gasps of air as she looked wide-eyed at the body.

"Oh, no," she whispered and looked at Jake and Arch for some type of comfort.

"Gather up the shit! Let's get the hell out of here!" Arch said as he looked around and brushed his long, black hair out of his face. He was trying to keep his composure the best he could, but he had fucked up, and he knew it.

They quickly left through the front door. That was a huge error, as the security camera discreetly placed above the door caught all three of their faces clear as day. Within twelve hours, the authorities knew exactly who they were.

Over the next few weeks, they were the most wanted people on the planet. Vanity and the idea that they were already in as much hot water as they could be pushed them to continue their crime spree. Unfortunately, two more people lost their lives in those weeks. One was a mother of three that Arch shot while robbing her parents' condo, and the other was a teenage boy who Jake hit with the aero car as they were fleeing yet another robbery.

As the authorities were beginning to close in on them, the options on the table were beginning to dwindle. They knew sooner or later they would be caught, maybe not all at once, but eventually, they all would. At one point or another, each one of them considered killing the others and going their own way. After all, dead men tell no tales. Before that plan could be implemented by any of them, Arch and Jake approached Tiggy with an idea. If they could find an orb, they could just leave the Gliese system and never look back. They had been researching places to hide, and Earth was one of the choices. All three of them knew a little bit about Earth culture, but they could learn more; my, yes, they certainly could.

Five days later, the three burst through the dome somewhere over Chile, and the trio blasted north toward New York. No alarms were raised thanks to an active cloaking device on the orb, something Colly had lacked on hers a few years earlier. Six hours later, they nonchalantly killed a man in New Jersey, stole his car, and drove into Manhattan via the Lincoln Tunnel.

It was in short order that the feds discovered the orb in a small patch of woods behind an elementary school in Belleville, New Jersey. They stuck with the story that the orb was actually an engine from a top-secret, experimental aircraft. Eventually, the orb was flown to Area 51 in Nevada, where it was stored in a secure hanger next to Colly's orb from two years earlier.

An hour later, the trio walked from below Brooklyn Bridge to the train station, where they took the subway to their newly rented apartment in Queens. Tiggy lifted the wallet of an elderly man next to her and bought pizzas for the crew. They sat in a circle on the dirty floor, ate pizza, and didn't say much.

Later that night, as they slept on the floor, Tiggy began to cry. She tried to hold back her sniffles.

"Oh, for fuck's sake!" Arch barked. "Stop crying!"

He kicked her in her thigh, hard. She muffled a little yelp and turned her face into the pillow. She cried into her pillow and tried her best to stay quiet.

Jake stood up and made his way to the bathroom. As he passed Tig, he gave her a little kick, too.

"Stop it, pussy," he mumbled.

She began having serious regrets about the life she was now living. Her future was shot, she was stuck on a strange planet, she had blood on her hands. It was a long time before she found sleep, and when she did, it was choppy and flooded with little nightmares.

4

Intergalactic Hideout. Allies. Project Starlight

THE LEAR TOUCHED DOWN AT DULLES AIRPORT right on schedule. This was surprising, considering the jet had made a stop in Dayton, Ohio, where a man in a black suit boarded the plane and handed the general a large envelope marked "Top Secret." Neither the general nor the man in black spoke. Five minutes later, the plane was blasting down the runway, continuing onto Dulles.

General Wallis was greeted by Lieutenant Bonilla, who snapped him a sharp salute as soon as he stepped off the plane.

"General, everything is in place, and they are waiting for you now," the lieutenant said as they walked quickly to the waiting sedan.

"Well, we're sure they are there, in New York," Wallis stated.

"Affirmative on them being there, sir, and as far as why, we are waiting to hear from Gliese to get some type of fix on what's going on. They seem reluctant to commit to any explanation at this point, other than the location of the orb. They tracked it as soon as it left Gliese." The lieutenant opened the door and they both slid in the back seat.

Wallis grunted, cracked the window, and lit a cigarette. "We can't have our planet used as an intergalactic hideout," he said frankly, almost irritated. "We need to nip this shit in the bud."

"I agree, sir. The joint chiefs of staff will concur as well," the lieutenant said.

Wallis drew a long drag from his cigarette and chuckled. "I have the response from Gliese."

"Oh?" Lieutenant Bonilla was surprised that the general hadn't told him that immediately.

"I read over it briefly. It's what I thought they might suggest," Wallis said.

The lieutenant nodded but inquired no further. He knew the general would eventually share the response with him and everyone concerned.

Fifty minutes later, they sat in a large and secure conference room on the third floor of a fairly nondescript building just two blocks from the White House. Although from its outward appearances, it may have looked like a run-of-the-mill office building, it was, in fact, a super-secure and clandestine meeting area for SETI and other intergalactic meetings and business.

Aside from General Wallis and Lieutenant Bonilla, the joint chiefs and secretary of defense also sat at the large table. There was a lot of small talk and niceties exchanged. Finally, General Wallis stood up.

"Gentlemen. You have all been briefed, and we all know why we are here. I think it's fair to say we are all on the same page with our feelings on this one."

Wallis opened up his briefcase and produced a large, plain, white envelope. He pulled the tab that read "Top Secret" and unfolded the single piece of paper.

"Gentlemen, this is from the council on Gliese. They have expressed their regrets for the three fugitives that have become parasites in New York. The letter goes on to offer a solution that they hope will satisfy all parties concerned."

All the men at the table leaned forward, awaiting the general's next words.

"They are offering to send two individuals to come here and relieve us of our … problem. Now, with that being said, I would like you gentlemen to keep an open mind and spirit here. We all know and are all familiar with who they want to send." The general smiled coldly and continued. "You are all familiar with Project Gemini?"

The men nodded.

"If you are not completely up to speed on it, Lieutenant Bonilla can fill you in with all the details. They are offering to have the two twins come here and fetch the criminals and return them to Gliese. They have promised the operation will be quick, low key, and safe for our citizens. Most importantly, this will keep our hands clean and out of the mix, should something go awry. The very last thing we need is to be involved in anything that may end up with the death of a Gliesen citizen, criminal or not; this is a chance we cannot take."

The group of men all nervously shifted in their seats.

Wallis continued. "Now, I know what a lot of you are thinking, and I can't say I don't agree with you. These girls killed a man in Central Park. An Earth man. Choked him to the point that his tongue was practically turned inside out. They killed a man, and that was unfortunate, but we cannot let that influence our decision. Gentlemen, this needs to be nipped in the bud like a cancer. We cannot allow these three fugitives to set up shop here. Period. More importantly, we cannot allow intergalactic fugitives to act carte blanche when it comes to using Earth as a refuge from their home planet's authorities."

In the end, they all agreed unanimously to allow the twins to return to Earth and retrieve the fugitive group, on the condition that there be an FBI agent to supervise them. Wallis announced that this top-secret project would be known as Project Starlight.

5

Robbery. Just an Earthling

ALL THE OLD MAN COULD TASTE WAS GUN OIL.
He tried to grunt and plead, but with the barrel of the snub-nose .22 in his mouth, he could only gasp. Instantly, he could feel one of his teeth floating around the barrel of the gun. He was sure his back teeth were broken, but he didn't feel any pain.

"You move, you die," Jake said. He pushed the barrel of the gun just a little bit farther into the old man's mouth.

Tig and Arch stood behind Jake and held a cash box that they had found under the man's bed next to a box of old photographs from the 1950s.

"Is there a key?" Tiggy asked nervously as she shook the box.

"Don't need one," Arch said and jerked the lockbox away from Tiggy.

The box was unlocked. Inside were a large wad of cash and a few pieces of vintage jewelry. At the very bottom were the old man's passport, birth certificate, and a few old stock certificates.

Arch jammed the cash and jewels into his pocket and dropped the lockbox on the bedroom floor, spilling the photographs and stock certificates on the carpet. The old man shook, and his wide eyes moved from side to side.

"Do it," Arch said coldly.

Suddenly, the back of the man's neck exploded out in a cascading red plume of blood, bone, and muscle. His body dropped to the floor in a heap and made a sickly thump as he hit the bedroom floor.

"Was this really necessary?" Tiggy yelled at the other two as she stared at the body.

"It's an earthling. Who gives a shit?" Jake said.

"Come on. Gather up anything you can carry in your pockets that we can sell quickly," Arch ordered. "We need cash, remember?"

The trio gathered up the spoils of the heist and left the apartment. On the way out, Jake opened the refrigerator and grabbed one of the old man's Blatz beers. He cracked the can and took a gulp.

"Here's to you, my friend," he mocked, toasting the mostly decapitated corpse of the kindly old man.

The trio gathered up the loot and slowly pushed open the door of the old man's brownstone, stuck their heads out, and walked quickly away into the New York night.

The next morning, the man's daughter came by to drop off a Crock-Pot of roast beef and found her father, or what was left of him, on the bedroom floor.

6

Dinner at Yellowjackets.
Visitors. Job Offer

COLLY AND JOSI STEPPED OFF THE TRAM, looked right and then left, and started the walk toward Yellowjackets bar. It was getting late, and the girls watched as the streetlights lit up one after another. For whatever reason, call it tuned minds, they both found the synchronicity of the lights turning on somewhat interesting and alluring.

"I hate going to this place." Josi pouted and kicked a discarded beer can out of her way.

"It's not that bad, Sis," Colly retorted. "Besides, would you rather go to one of those snooty-tooty restaurants on the beach where they stare at us like fish in a bowl?"

"Oh, they don't stare at us here?" Josi mumbled and hung her head low.

Ten minutes later, they walked into Yellowjackets and found a table in the crowded bar. Just as Josi said, most of the rough-looking patrons glanced at the twins and stared a little longer than they should.

Seconds later, a gum-snapping waitress approached the table and took their drink order: a beer for Josi and ginger ale with a splash of lemonade for Colly.

"Are you going to eat?" Josi asked.

"If you are, I am," Colly said and looked nonchalantly around the bar.

A minute later, the waitress patiently took their orders, and the girls smiled and handed back the menus. They sighed in unison and looked at each other.

"We need to talk about this," Colly said and looked at Josi.

Josi nodded and took a swig of her beer. "We do."

Earlier that day, Colly had gone to the market and picked up the things she needed, including Josi's powdered sugar and dark chocolate, and returned home. She spent an hour or so going over blueprints for a new office complex project she was an advisor on and spoke to the construction people on the phone.

Later that afternoon, just before dinner, Josi came back over, and the twins sat down at the kitchen table and chatted lightly. Josi told Colly about the parents of a child in her class that seemed to have it in for her. Nobody knew that Josi was an earthling, but from time to time, she was able to Blush that some people sensed that something was off with her. Not that Josi cared in the slightest.

As they sat at the table, sipping their coffee and dishing, both girls felt a very slight twinge in their heads—a buzzing like a hive of bees that someone had poked with a stick. They looked at each other instantly, their coffee cups frozen in their hands mid-sip.

"Did you feel that?" Josi said, slightly alarmed.

"Uh-huh. What is it?" Colly said nervously.

Josi was about to speak when there was a loud knock at the door. Both girls looked toward the door and then back at each other, puzzled.

"I guess that answers that," Colly said and smiled slightly.

"Should we answer it?" Josi said.

"You go. I'll wait here," Colly said and shifted in her seat.

"Shit. Okay," Josi said as she stood up and walked to the big, glass front door.

Josi took a deep breath and quickly swung the door open. She was met by four stern, stony-faced men in military uniforms.

"Colly?" Josi called over her shoulder. "It's for you."

Minutes later, the small group sat in Colly's living room while Josi handed out drinks to all the men and her sister. Everyone was politely introduced, and she sat down close to Josi, as if they were comforting one another.

"So, I know you're not here to see the gorgeous view from my balcony," Colly said dryly and looked at each of the men individually.

"That's entirely correct," replied the man who introduced himself as General Rhea, commander of the National Police Commission.

General Rhea spoke with authority and conviction. As he spoke, Josi thought to herself that he looked as if he was chiseled out of limestone. In a quick flash of immaturity, she wondered if his cock was also chiseled out of rock.

Over the next fifteen minutes, the general and his cohorts explained to the girls in detail how three Gliesen fugitives were able to escape the planet and flee to Earth, where they were now living and, unfortunately, continuing their crime spree. The general went into great detail about how they had shot and killed a major in the guard and how he had a two-year-old daughter that was now fatherless. He briefed them on the others they had killed and lives they had ruined. The twins listened with curious interest.

"I hate to ask the obvious," Colly said, "but how do you know they went to Earth? How do you know they aren't on another planet or hiding out in the basement of one of their friends' houses here on Gliese?"

Rhea smiled, nodded, and glanced at the other men. "The orb was clandestinely tracked as soon as they left Gliese. We thought Earth was their likely destination, and we were correct."

Josi chimed in. "I hate to also point out the obvious, but why is this any of our concern? Why can't the police on Earth handle this? What can't you handle this? I mean, why are you here telling us about this?"

"I can't go into as much detail as you, or I, for that matter, would like, but our relationship with Earth is solid, and our agreements are clear. This is *our* problem. These fugitives are *our* embarrassment. This is *our* mess, and we are going to clean it up. We spilled milk in their kitchen, and we don't expect them to mop it up."

The twins looked at each other and Josi spoke, narrowing her eyes. "Don't you mean *we* are going to clean it up? I mean, why should we?"

General Rhea sighed and leaned forward. Just as he was about to speak, a voice from across the room chimed in, startling the small group in the living room.

"How about your instinct to do the right thing?"

Everyone in the living room stood up and faced the man who had silently slipped in the front door and who was now standing in the doorway of the big living room. Josi and Colly stayed seated and looked at each other comically.

"Pancros," General Rhea said, surprised. "We did not expect you."

Pancros ignored him and began walking into the living room.

"Leave us, please," he said.

Instantly, General Rhea and his small entourage walked quickly out of the room toward the front door without saying a word. Pancros stood still until he heard the front door shut, and then he smiled at the twins.

"Please, sit down," he said to the girls.

The three sat in silence for a moment until finally, Pancros spoke.

"You two … you look like your mother."

Colly sat emotionless, her poker face in prime form. "You knew our mother?"

"I did," he said as he eyed the girls closely. "She was a wonderful woman. The resemblance is quite remarkable."

Pancros looked at Josi. "How has your adjustment been to Gliese? No problems, from what I understand."

Josi raised her eyebrows but stayed silent. She was sure Pancros wanted her to know he had been keeping track of her and, most likely, Colly.

Pancros sighed. "My colleague, General Rhea, has no doubt filled you in on our slight problem."

"Slight problem?" Colly said and smiled.

Josi, who knew her sister was gearing up for a confrontation, thought deeply and whispered into her sister's head, *Colly, shush your face.*

Pancros leaned forward and smiled. "Yes, Colly, shush your face."

Both girls dropped their jaws.

"Fuck," Colly said.

Pancros leaned back and smiled gently. "Don't worry, girls. My ... Blush ... isn't nearly as strong as yours. I barely heard you, and the only reason I did was because I'm so close to you."

Josi crossed her arms. "What do you want?"

"We want you to go to Earth and retrieve the three criminals," Pancros stated quickly, with an air of surprise. "Certainly, Rhea filled you in on the violence these three have done, correct?"

"He did, but why us? We asked him why the police on Earth don't just arrest them and send them back here," Josi replied.

"It's not quite that simple. Josi, you, for one, should know that people on Earth are largely unaware of life outside of their own planet. In order to capture these ... people ... the earthlings would have to brief a large number of people; the logistics would be immense, and more than likely, everyone involved would be a little too chatty. No, our best bet is to send the two of you to Earth. This way, we can keep it as simple and confined as we can."

Pancros sighed and continued. "Certainly, you two have noticed you are far from typical Gliesen beings. Do you think everyone can do the things that you do? Are you under the illusion that everyone can talk to each other in their heads at will? That everyone can sense things? Your mother ... she was a great Star Warrior ... and so are you two."

Both Josi and Colly sat blank-faced as they absorbed what they were being told. Perhaps now, being told without question that they were Star Children, had solidified what they had already known. They were not like the others.

"You two … you are just now discovering what you are capable of. As time goes by, your sense of perception and telepathy will grow. You have already far exceeded what anyone else can do. Time will sharpen you even more."

Pancros looked at Colly and then Josi. "Let me be even more frank. You both got a pass on your last field trip to Earth. Not everyone was pleased with that, and some of us took a great deal of criticism for it. Now the same people who understand your need to break laws and find each other are asking for your help. That's it. Can we count on you?"

In the end, the twins knew they had to go. Pancros was right; they should have been having this conversation from inside a detention cell, but they weren't. This, compounded by a strange internal ache that seemed to be pushing them toward an unknown destiny, gave them a little and final nudge.

7

Andy. Top Secret.
Big News. X-Files

SPECIAL AGENT ANDY CECA WAS SITTING AT his desk at the FBI field office in Manhattan, shuffling through a stack of papers when his phone rang.

"Ceca," he said casually and then put the paper down and glanced up at the clock on the wall.

"Hey, Andy," the voice on the other end of the line said casually. "Can you run down to fourteen? There are a couple white collars from Washington who want to talk to you."

Andy raised his eyebrows. "Me? What for?" he asked.

"I didn't ask, and I got the feeling they wouldn't tell," the voice said and chuckled.

"Okay. I'll be down in five minutes. Should I bring anything?"

"No. Not as far as I know," the voice said and hung up.

Special Agent Ceca walked out of the glass office he shared with four other agents and headed down the hall to the elevator banks. Just before he got to the elevator, he decided to hit the head first. After he had done his business, he stood in front of the sink, washed his hands, and took a long look at himself in the mirror. At twenty-five years old, he was one of the younger agents at the Manhattan field office. He was unmarried and had no close family to speak of. He did have a brother in Iowa that sold computers, but they rarely spoke, and both of his parents had passed away years ago. Andy was basically on his own. This wasn't a big problem for him, being a solitary person by nature. Even in a city like New York, he found it easy to keep to himself.

At the bureau, he excelled and found himself on special assignment investigating unsolved murders containing hints of the occult. This was an assignment that Andy found curiously interesting, and his closure rate on his cases was extremely high—something that pleased his superiors to no end. He had countless certificates on the wall in his Brooklyn apartment and had even won the J. Edgar Hoover award for excellence.

He ran a comb through his sandy-blond hair and fixed his tie. He was a tall man at six feet, and his broad shoulders screamed authority. He had the stereotypical FBI face and posture: good-looking and authoritative. What most people didn't know about Andy was that outside of the office, stripped of his FBI armor, he was a funny and casual guy. He was a huge Mets fan and cycled the city every chance he got. He liked to paint abstract art, and on Sunday mornings, he volunteered at the local soup kitchen. In his apartment, he had a growing collection of books about UFOs, Sasquatch, and the occult.

While he was in his second year at the FBI Academy, he was privileged to look at old case files that had long gone cold. One file that caught his attention concerned an eighteen-year-old female who was reportedly abducted by a Bigfoot outside a restaurant in Kendall, Washington. The witness who had seen the actual abduction was the busboy at the bar who was taking out the trash at closing time when he heard screams coming from the small dirt parking lot in back. He witnessed the girl being dragged into the woods by her leg by what he described as an eight-foot-tall Sasquatch. The local PD and state police scratched their heads and did their due diligence in solving the case. They turned up nothing, even with a massive search party and bloodhounds, and the case continued to perplex those involved. Forty-five years later, the case was still unsolved.

That case had always bothered Andy, and as he read through all the witness reports and backgrounds of those involved, he was struck by a little note scribbled in the corner of one of the papers. It simply read:

"Homeowner on Dardu Road is said to have seen lights in the sky at the time of the disappearance."

Andy pushed open the lavatory door with his shoulder, walked to the elevators, and pushed the down button. Once the door opened with a gentle swish, he stepped in and hit the button for the fourteenth floor.

A few quick seconds later, he stepped out of the elevator, looked left and then right, and walked the short distance to the conference room. He fixed his tie once more and stepped inside.

"Special Agent Ceca, graduate of the FBI Academy and top of the class to boot," Wallis said as he lit a cigarette and scanned Andy's personal file. "You did a paper on Project Blue Book that raised a lot of eyebrows. Your theory on deep-sea extraterrestrials was quite interesting." Wallis paused. His mouth showed just a hint of a smile. "It's also my understanding that you consider yourself somewhat of an amateur UFO hunter. Is that true?"

"Yes, sir. I also hunt for Bigfoot and other cryptids." Andy shrugged and grinned.

Wallis looked pleased and motioned for Andy to sit down. Wallis, Andy, and Lieutenant Bonilla were all now seated at the table.

"Agent Ceca, what I'm about to tell you might shock you, or it may not. It goes without saying that this conversation is above top secret and for your ears only. Do you understand, Agent Ceca?"

"Yes, sir. Of course, I understand." Andy sat up straight and cleared his throat.

Wallis looked at Lieutenant Bonilla quickly and then began speaking as if it were a rehearsed speech.

"Agent Ceca." Wallis took a deep drag of his cigarette. "Since the 1950s, our government and other select governments around the globe have been aware of, and have had a relationship with, alien life forms from other planets. One of our closest allies is a species on the planet Gliese. Since 1968, we have been on diplomatic terms, and our relationship has been mutually beneficial."

Wallis looked closely at Andy and tried to read his emotions, but Andy kept his poker face. He continued.

"As you might guess, there is only so much I can tell you. I *can* tell you this, though. We are now faced with a situation that requires our involvement and cooperation with the Gliesen government. Last month, a trio of fugitives left Gliese and are now in New York City. They committed murder on their home planet, and we think at least one, possibly two human deaths can be traced back to them here on Earth. Now, the council on Gliese has offered to send two ... hunters to Earth to capture and return the fugitives back to Gliese to stand trial. You are being tasked with the assignment to work with and assist them in their pursuit of the three outlaws."

Andy did his best to keep his emotions in check. He was shocked and fascinated with what the general was telling him. He knew not to ask too many questions and to try to keep his poker face. He needed to ask a few basic questions, but he didn't want to look too eager or shocked. One thing he knew was that these bigwig military types played their cards close to the vest and even if he did ask questions, he probably wouldn't get answers.

"General, is there a timeline here? Exactly how am I supposed to help them? Who are they?"

Lieutenant Bonilla looked at General Wallis and spoke firmly. "The operation will begin within the next day or so, and their names are Josi and Colly. Josi spent most of her life in New York and has been living on Gliese for the past two years or so. Colly is her twin sister and spent her entire life on Gliese. It shouldn't concern you any farther than that, Agent Ceca."

Andy nodded; he wanted to ask a million questions. His head was spinning, and he felt like everything that he had always suspected was now true. It was obvious that the lieutenant and Wallis both sensed this, but they didn't act upon it.

"They will be at Area 51 in Nevada tomorrow and in New York in the next day or so." Lieutenant Bonilla glanced at Wallis and continued.

"For the most part, they are on cruise control. Your job is to guide them on earthly matters. Directions, locations ... shit, the best subway to take. That kinda thing. From what we understand, you grew up in Brooklyn and know the city inside and out. Hell, we know you drove a cab in college."

General Wallis chimed in. "Agent Ceca, under no circumstances are you to participate in the capture of the fugitives. Leave that to Colly and Josi. We can't have an earthling killing one of these fugitives, unless an earthling's life is in direct danger. So basically, stay clear. Is that perfectly clear?"

"It is," Andy stated.

General Wallis slid a file across the table to Andy. Marked on the side of the folder in clear, typeset print was: "Top Secret. SETI/ NORAD Eyes Only." Andy looked at both the lieutenant and General Wallis and then slowly opened the file. The first thing he saw was an 8x10 photograph of the twins. The photograph was provided by the Gliesen government and showed the girls sitting next to each other and looking directly into the camera. It was an undercover shot of the twins taken just a week ago. The photo was stunning, and Andy had a hard time looking away. The girl on the left side of the picture, the girl with the white hair, took his breath away.

"Whoa," Andy said under his breath. "These two are law enforcement?"

"Not exactly," Bonilla said. "They are, from what we've been told, equipped to handle this better than any police officer possibly could."

General Wallis stood up. "Agent Ceca, that's all for now. Lieutenant Bonilla here will be in touch tomorrow with the rest of the details and get you on a plane to Nevada. And Agent Ceca ... welcome to Project Starlight."

Later that night, in his Brooklyn apartment, Andy smiled as he watched reruns of *The X-Files* with the lights off.

8

Yummy Dinner.
I Miss Hell's Kitchen

BACK AT YELLOWJACKETS BAR, THE GIRLS enjoyed their meals of spaghetti and meatballs while they talked about the events of that afternoon.

"He's holding something back. I can feel it, Colly."

Colly nodded while she spun her spaghetti on her fork.

"I know. I could feel it too, but he is clever and is hiding it well."

"Do you think we can do this? I mean seriously, Colly. I'm a teacher, and you're a fuckin' engineer. What makes them, or us, think we can hunt down these three hardened criminals?" Josi asked as she pulled little pieces off her dinner roll and tossed them in her mouth.

"Josi-bear, relax. We both know we can do this. We both know we're different. On Earth, we can hunt down anyone, if we want to. Pancros is right about one thing: our abilities are growing. On Earth, who knows what we can feel?"

"Then you want to go?" Josi asked.

"Yes, Josi, I do. Besides, the three they want us to find are really bad people. They killed all those people! They left those poor kids without a father." Colly sighed. "And you'd get to go back to Earth, right?"

Josi smiled, just a little, at the thought of returning to New York. Maybe she hadn't been completely honest with her sister when asked if she missed Earth. She did. Not in any deep and meaningful way, but in the way a tourist might miss a place they really loved on a road trip. She missed Hell's Kitchen. She missed the smell of her neighborhood and the sounds of Manhattan. She missed the way the city pulsated under her feet as she walked along Seventh Avenue. She missed her little apartment and her neighbor, Mrs. Cocca.

"I guess I would like to go back and have a look around," Josi said as she craned her neck and looked for the waitress. She wanted more bread.

"Then it's settled. We'll go back, take care of this thing, take a little trip to Hell's Kitchen, and then back home. Easy breezy," Colly said.

Josi looked at her, troubled. "Yeah, right, easy breezy."

9

Troubles of Our Own

"I'M SO FUCKIN' BORED I COULD KILL MYSELF,"
Tiggy said as she looked out the window of their third-story apartment in Queens. She gazed upward as a Delta jet flew overhead, headed into LaGuardia.

"Then why don't you?" Arch asked. He flipped through the television stations as he chain-smoked cigarettes.

"Fuck off," Tig mumbled.

The pair sat in their rented apartment in the Jackson Heights neighborhood of Queens. The third, Jake, had been MIA since yesterday morning, and despite the nonchalant swaggers from Tiggy and Arch, they were worried.

Jake being gone could mean a plethora of bad things—mostly, that he had been caught. Whether by Earth officials or Gliese, it didn't matter. Caught was caught.

They were well aware that just because they were on Earth, they may not be safe from the long arm of Gliesen justice. Tiggy had a constant look of fear and concern on her face and just that morning, she had noticed several clumps of her red hair floating on the pillow. Her heart beat just a little faster than normal, and her stomach ached and burned.

As if on cue, the apartment door swung open, and Jake stumbled in, laughing. It was instantly clear that Jake was drunk.

"Where in the fuck have you been?" Tiggy snapped and turned toward him.

"Oh, out and about." Jake laughed and stumbled to the couch.

Tiggy walked quickly toward him and shoved Jake hard. He fell backward onto the old couch and began laughing.

"Fuck off!" Tiggy screamed in his face. The scotch fumes rolled off his tongue, which made Tiggy gag.

"Enough, you two! We need money, and we need a plan," Arch said as he grabbed Tiggy by the neck and shoved her away from Jake.

"Nope," Jake said. "All taken care of, my fine friends."

Jake dug deep into his pockets and started pulling out handfuls of cash. His grin never faltered as the money went from his pockets onto the cheap coffee table. Piles of twenty- and fifty-dollar bills littered the table, some spilling onto the floor.

"Where did you get all this?" Tiggy asked, concerned.

"This is New York City, baby! You know, start spreading the news and all that funky shit!" Jake laughed drunkenly.

Arch stepped forward and looked down at Jake. His fists and teeth were clenched. "I hope you didn't do anything reckless, my friend."

Jake shook his head and he lay down on the couch. His eyes closed, and he was out. Tig and Arch stood over him, and they both looked worried.

10

Back to Earth. Why, Hello! Doughnuts

JOSI AND COLLY WERE CRAMPED IN THE ORB as it cut through the black holes of time and space on its way to Earth. The sisters were clad in their earthly space goggles, and Josi clutched her Yankees cap. As they blasted through space and twisted time, they elbowed each other as they looked for more room. The orb punched through the dome somewhere over Alaska, and in an instant, the twins turned the orb south toward Nevada. They sped up to Mach 3 and smiled and laughed as they held on.

Just as they crossed into Nevada, Colly slowed considerably and mischievously rolled the orb inverted. They both laughed hysterically as they continued their dash through Nevada, upside down.

"Colly, flip us back over!" Josi screamed while holding tight to her Yankees cap.

Just as she said that, the orb dropped several thousand feet. They were still inverted, and both girls tried to get to the control pad to fix the problem. Colly smacked Josi's hand away from the control pad as she righted the orb.

"Josi, hang on!" Colly yelled and then laughed and held onto her seat. The orb hit the desert floor and skidded to a stop on the tarmac not far from the group of waiting officials who were anxious to meet and greet the extraterrestrial twins.

Colly smashed a large button by the door to open the craft. Both girls rolled out of the orb in a heap and lay tangled on the desert floor. They both giggled as they tried to stand up.

They stopped instantly and looked up from the sandy ground. A group of stern officials stared down in disbelief.

"Ummmm ... hi!" Colly said and slipped off her goggles and helped Josi stand up. Josi quickly lifted her sister's goggles, and they both stood up straight. They, of course, towered over the group of men, who now smiled nervously up at them.

"So, you must be Josi and Colly," General Wallis said as he reached his hand out for both Colly and Josi to shake.

"Yes! I'm Colly, and this is my sister Josi." The girls looked around nervously at their new environment.

"Shall we get going? We have a few things to cover. Are you girls hungry? Can we get you anything?" The general was uncharacteristically accommodating.

"I can eat," Colly said rather matter-of-factly while she brushed herself off. Josi nodded in agreement with her sister and smiled.

They made their way in a small caravan of military jeeps to a rounded, metal Quonset-like building in a fairly large compound of other structures, including several hangers. As the girls stepped out of the jeep, Colly nudged Josi and looked at an Air Force F-15 fighter in one of the hangers.

"Cool," Colly said as she sidestepped and made a beeline for the fighter.

Josi pulled her arm and got her back in line.

Once inside, the group of military and civilian advisors all sat down in an air-conditioned conference room. Two enlisted men brought out trays of food for the group. Colly looked at the tray of blueberry doughnuts and grabbed two with strange curiosity. Josi smiled out of the corner of her eye, knowing Colly had never had a doughnut.

Wallis stood up and began to speak. "I know you've been briefed about the situation from the Gliesen Council, and frankly, we don't have a lot to add. Ladies, this is FBI Agent Andy Ceca."

Andy stood up and nodded at the twins. His gaze held just a second longer at Josi. Colly noticed and smiled with her cheeks puffed out with blueberry doughnut.

"Agent Ceca will be at your disposal for the duration. He will not be participating in the operation directly, but he will be there to assist you in anything else. Consider him your earthly liaison," Wallis said.

Colly nudged Josi under the table and smiled. In retort, Josi pinched her sister on the leg. Colly smiled painfully as she continued to stuff doughnuts in her mouth. She gave her sister a furtive kick under the table.

General Wallis and Andy looked at each other nervously as the twins had their little exchange.

"I'm looking forward to helping in any way that I can. Josi, I was told you are from New York," Andy said.

Josi nodded brightly. "I am … I was. Hell's Kitchen. I was a teacher at PS 51."

"I live in Brooklyn. Bay Ridge," Andy said and smiled at her.

Colly turned, and with her mouth full of doughnut, she whispered in her sister's ear. "You two would probably have lots to talk about."

Josi shot her sister a sly look, turned to Andy, and said politely, "Tony Manaro, eh?"

Right away, Andy got the pop-culture reference. His eyes crinkled as he grinned at Josi.

General Wallis and the rest of the officials looked at each other with raised eyebrows, not getting the joke.

"Well, there's a plane waiting for us. I suggest we get moving. Colly, Josi, any questions for us?' Wallis asked.

The girls shook their heads, as everyone stood up and began walking toward the door. Colly took her time and stood up slowly. As soon as all backs were turned, she grabbed two more doughnuts and shoved them in her mouth.

11

Silly Girl, Colly. Amelia Earhart

AN HOUR LATER, A LEAR C-21 WAS CRUISING
at twenty-eight thousand feet on its way from Las Vegas to Teterboro,
New Jersey. Colly and Josi were crammed into the seats and visibly
uncomfortable. Their six-foot, three-inch statures were cumbersome
inside the small jet.

Accompanying them were General Wallis, Professor Raptis from
SETI, two young NASA Scientists, and Agent Ceca. They snuck glances
at the girls. Both the sisters largely ignored the looks as they shared and
read a day-old Las Vegas newspaper. From time to time, Josi would raise
her eyes over the paper and steal a glance at Andy.

Colly began to fidget and elbow Josi, looking for more room. Josi
elbowed her back and shot her a dirty look.

Colly glared back at her sister and exhaled loudly. She slowly slid
out of her tight seat and began slowly crawling up the aisle on her hands
and knees. Josi covered her mouth to hold back a giggle. Colly's hips
swung in big arches from side to side as she crawled up to the cockpit.
People on both sides of the aisle leaned out to see what the hell this girl
was up to.

She peered into the cockpit, taking the young pilots by surprise.

"Go faster," Colly said and smiled.

"This is about all she's got, ma'am," the co-pilot said and looked
down at her, perplexed.

Colly reached up from her hands and knees and pushed the
throttles forward. The plane lurched slightly, and an alarm went
off while the cockpit dashboard lit up. In the back of the plane, the

passengers tilted to the left and reached for anything to hold onto. The pilots immediately pushed her hand away and adjusted the throttles. The pilot in command shot her an angry glare.

"That's enough of that, little lady."

Colly smiled and immediately reached up to push something on the autopilot, ignoring the pilot-in-command's orders. The co-pilot pushed her hand away firmly.

"Jesus, lady, stop playing around! Shit." Colly pouted.

Josi sighed and smiled. She stood up and moved forward, hunched over, to get Colly. She grabbed Colly by the scruff of her hair and pulled her back.

"Hey!" Colly barked. "Ouch! Josi, that hurts!"

Josi hid her smile. "Come on, Amelia Earhart."

Colly turned her body around and shuffled on her knees back to her seat. "Who the hell is Amelia Earhart?"

Two uncomfortable hours later, the jet touched down in New Jersey and taxied to a private hangar on the outskirts of Teterboro Airport. Waiting were three plain, unmarked sedans that took the entourage to an FBI field office on Twenty-Third Street in Manhattan.

During the twenty-minute ride into Manhattan, Josi looked out the car's tinted back window in excitement, while Colly remarked nonchalantly as they went through the Lincoln Tunnel that back on Gliese, she had given an old boyfriend a hand job in a tunnel much like this one. The young Air Force driver looked at Colly in the rearview mirror with a raised eyebrow. Colly met his eyes in the mirror, shrugged, and winked.

Once they arrived at FBI headquarters, they spent the next hour or so going over the logistics of the operation. Both Colly and Josi found all the planning a little overwhelming and even perhaps slightly unnecessary. They listened politely and asked a few questions about local laws and other formalities. Finally, General Wallis opened his briefcase and pulled out a manila folder.

"These are the individuals you are looking for," he said as he shared pictures of the three fugitives: Tiggy, Arch, and Jake. The photos were provided by the council on Gliese.

"From what we've been told, Arch is the unspoken leader. Apparently, he's the one that's calling the shots." Wallis pointed to the photo of Arch.

The girls looked at the pictures for a minute and then slid them back to Wallis. They had been shown the same photos on Gliese.

Colly sighed and asked, "Do you have any leads at all as to where they might be hiding? Anything at all?"

"No, I'm afraid not." Wallis shook his head.

Josi started to stand up. She leaned into her sister and said quietly, "Relax, Sis. We'll find them."

She then looked at General Wallis and announced that they would start the day after tomorrow.

Wallis and Lieutenant Bonilla looked at each other. "That will be fine. I'm sorry there isn't more to go on, but New York is a big place," Wallis said.

The twins nodded and smiled.

"No worries. We'll get them," Colly said slyly.

12

Tummy Problems.
Pizza for Dinner

THE US GOVERNMENT HAD GRACIOUSLY gotten the girls a beautiful suite at the Plaza Hotel, a place that Colly and Josi were familiar with. As the girls walked through the lobby, Colly mischievously looked around for her old friend Carrie but didn't see her. As they stood by the elevator waiting, Josi looked at her sister.

"You okay, Colly girl?"

"Uh-huh, kinda. My tummy hurts a little from those doughnuts blueberries I ate."

Josi smiled at her sister. "They're called blueberry doughnuts, not doughnuts blueberry. Besides, I guess I should have told you not to eat six of them."

Colly ignored her and stepped into the elevator. The door swished shut and Josi pressed the button to their floor.

"Everyone seemed nice at the meeting," Josi said, trying to make small talk while watching her sister with concern.

Colly ignored her; she looked very uncomfortable.

"Colly, what's wrong? You look horrible," Josi asked and looked her sister up and down.

The elevator door swished open, and Colly pushed her way out and ran down the hall to their suite. She slid the key card in the slot, and with a little beep, the door clicked open, and Colly ran for the bathroom.

Josi followed behind her and yelled through the closed bathroom door. "Are you okay?"

Colly moaned. "No! My stomach! Stupid fuckin' bluedoughs or whatever the fuck you call them!"

Josi covered her mouth and giggled. "Colly! Jesus, Colly! You should have stopped at one!"

Colly just moaned.

"Hey! This is really nice!' Josi said excitedly as she walked into the living room and looked over their digs for the next couple days.

Colly continued to moan from the bathroom, which made Josi grin.

An hour later, feeling no worse for wear, Colly sat on the bed flipping through the channels on the television, while Josi looked out the window and scanned the city.

"Can you eat?" Josi asked.

"Yeah, I think so. Can we get pizza?" Colly asked, perking up instantly.

"We sure can. Green peppers and mushrooms cool?" Josi asked.

"Yep, yep," Colly said. "Get some of that Grape Crush stuff, too."

In short order, the twins were scarfing down pizza. The conversation was light and airy, and they tossed around ideas about what they could do tomorrow for fun. They allowed themselves a day to play before they rolled up their sleeves and got to the task at hand. They didn't talk about the upcoming job, and maybe that was a good thing. They didn't need to think and submerge themselves in the upcoming tasks too much. They were both cautiously confident that they would be able to find and capture all three. They were also aware that nothing was guaranteed, and perhaps the three fugitives were more clever than they were giving them credit for.

As they got ready for bed that night, they stopped as they turned down the bed and looked at each other.

Colly thought deeply. *Are you ready for this?*

Yeah, I think so. Colly, I'm worried, though. I want this badly.

Colly didn't think back. Instead, she took a deep breath and spoke out loud. "Don't worry, Sis. It's the right thing to do. They are very, very bad people."

"I love you." Josi looked at her Gemini and smiled.

"I love you, too, Sis," Colly said as she turned off the light.

13

A New Plan. Three Blind Mice

AS COLLY AND JOSI RELAXED IN THEIR SUITE at the Plaza, Agent Ceca and General Wallis sat in a dimly lit conference room at the FBI field office in Manhattan.

"So, what are your thoughts?" Wallis asked Andy while he ate his takeout Chinese food.

Andy leaned back in his chair and sipped his soda. "I don't know. Hard to get a fix on those two. Of course, my impression is that they might be far more capable than they look. I've read the files on them. They sure did a number on Robert Underwood a few years back."

Wallis nodded while he adjusted his chopsticks. "That was unfortunate, but Mr. Underwood wasn't exactly a model citizen. He would have killed sooner or later; they just stopped him before he could."

Andy shrugged and nodded. "Now we are sending them out into the city to perhaps kill again. At the meeting and all the briefings, I don't remember you, or anyone for that matter, telling the twins *not* to kill them. You never said, 'dead or alive,' right?"

Wallis wiped his mouth slowly with his napkin and leaned forward. "Listen, Andy ... the three fugitives are Gliese's problem, not ours. Yes, they are here on Earth. Yes, they have more than likely killed an earthling. Yes, they are a drain on our resources. But understand, Andy; they are not earthlings, they are Gliese, and we are in a good position to strengthen our ties with the council there. If we play ball now, perhaps in the future, they will play ball with us."

Wallis lit a cigarette and continued. "We have a very good idea of what the twins are capable of. So, what if we could use them? What if we gave them access to the most complex crimes on Earth that have eluded us? What if we gave them free reign to work for *us*?"

Andy thought deeply. "Is that possible? Have you spoken to the council on Gliese about this? Certainly, they would want something in return, right?"

"It was … discussed lightly, I guess you can say." Wallis cleared his throat and continued. "You're right; they would almost certainly want something in return. It certainly opens up a lot of possibilities, right? Think about it. Right now, we have a killer running around the city of Pittsburgh who takes pleasure in cutting out the eyes of his victims. The police and our agents in Pittsburgh are stumped. This guy has a body count that is growing exponentially. There's another nut in Iowa that uses the massive cornfields as his hunting grounds. He makes these strange crosses out of corn and ties his victims to them. What if we sent the girls on a little trip to Pittsburgh or Iowa? Understand?"

Andy did understand. It was becoming clear to him that the United States Government had a secondary plan to use the girls to hunt down the most dangerous people in the country.

Andy leaned back in his chair and exhaled. "Are you opening Pandora's Box with this plan, General?"

"That, Agent Ceca, shall remain to be seen," Wallis said with a chuckle.

14

Bronx Bound. Josi Has a Crush

THE FIRST FULL DAY BACK IN NEW YORK CITY was a packed schedule of fun for the twins. Despite the constant, nagging thoughts of the hunt in the back of their minds, they were both set on enjoying the day before they got down to the most unpleasant business of apprehending the trio of outlaws. With almost deliberate cause, they pushed the sprinkles of Blush away and enjoyed New York.

They spent the late morning and early afternoon bopping and shopping around the Big Apple. The day was warm and sunny, without a cloud in the sky.

This was the first time Colly had been able to truly absorb New York City for what it was, and she loved it. More than once, Josi had to tug at her arm and pull her along as she looked up at the amazing architecture of the old, historic buildings in the city.

They walked the Brooklyn Bridge and shopped in Soho for clothes. Colly took tons of pictures, and they bought matching New York Yankees jerseys. Colly bought a new stocking cap, while Josi bought pink jeans and a new black scarf.

As they strolled hand in hand along Canal Street and Third Avenue, a man doing magic tricks on the sidewalk immediately caught their attention. The small crowd was enthralled as he shuffled cards and tossed coins. Josi and Colly stood toward the back; they towered over the small crowd. Of course, they knew all the tricks and how the clever street magician did them. Josi watched Colly out of the corner of her eye. She knew Colly was about to put on a show and upstage the street magician on a level he would never see coming, but as soon as Colly started to step through the small crowd, Josi grabbed her arm and pulled her back. Colly stumbled backward. She didn't peek deep enough into the magician. Had she, she would have seen his son with leukemia and a family that needed every penny it could get, no matter how the dad got it.

"Leave him alone, sweetheart," Josi said and squeezed her sister's hand.

Colly looked at her sister for a brief second and smiled. Josi smiled back. Colly got it.

As the afternoon pressed on, they made their way back to the Plaza Hotel via Madison Avenue. The crowds stared as usual, and also as usual, Colly made faces while Josi laughed.

As dinner approached, the pair ordered another mushroom-and-green-pepper pizza and watched television in their suite at the Plaza. After supper, Josi announced that they were going out. Colly jumped up and down like a small child on Christmas.

"Where are we going?" she asked excitedly.

Josi giggled and teased, "Who wants to go to see the Yankees?"

Colly did a little happy dance. "The Yankees? Really? Me! I want to go! Me! Me! Me!"

"Go put on your Yankees jersey," Josi said and watched Colly beam.

Colly jumped over the sofa in a single bound and ran into the bedroom; she tore through the bags of clothes they had bought earlier that day. She laughed and shouted questions about baseball to Josi. She found the jerseys at the bottom of an "I Love NY" bag, tore off her shirt, and slipped the jersey on.

"Put mine on the bed, will you?" Josi yelled as she finished her last piece of pizza and gulped Grape Crush.

"Should I wear jeans or shorts?" Colly yelled.

Josi peeked into the bedroom. "Wear jeans; it can get chilly."

An hour later, they were on the train heading into the Bronx. Both sisters were incredibly excited to see the Yanks, and Josi could barely sit still on the train.

Josi had splurged and gotten tickets behind the Yankees dugout. The girls were more of an attraction to the people sitting around them than the game was. Colly screamed at every play and jumped up and down whenever the Yankees got a hit. The fans, and even a few of the players, stared at them in reserved disbelief.

During the seventh-inning stretch, the Yankee shortstop tossed Colly a ball. Colly tossed it back. The famous shortstop grinned and lobbed it back to Colly, who immediately threw it back. The exasperated player tossed it back again. Josi grabbed the ball and yelled, "Thank you!" She explained to her sister that it was called a souvenir and it was meant for her to keep.

They had a blast, and by the time they got back to the hotel, they were hoarse from screaming and buzzed from the beers they had smashed.

Later that night, they lay in bed on their backs next to each other and stared up at the ceiling. Colly held the baseball in her hand and turned it over and over. The whites of their eyes were visible in the dim light of the hotel suite.

"Are you nervous about tomorrow?" Colly asked.

"Kinda. I mean, I'm not sure what's supposed to happen. It's weird; I feel like we have a new cog in our mental gears. An instinct to hunt. Do you feel it?"

"I do, Josi. I can smell them," Colly said with a slight tone of disgust in her voice.

"Me too," Josi said with a sigh.

After a minute of silence where the only sound was the faint howl of sirens and car horns, Colly smiled to herself.

"You like Andy, don't you?" Colly nudged her. "I can tell you do. I saw you looking at him yesterday at the meeting. He is a cutie patootie."

"Go kick a dick," Josi mumbled and rolled over, away from her sister.

Colly giggled, leaned over, put her new baseball on the nightstand, and switched the bed light off. She moved her sister's hair away from her face and kissed her cheek, then curled up tight next to her and closed her eyes.

That night, as the dream cycle wrapped itself around them and squeezed, they dreamt the same dream—the dream of the hunt.

15

Let the Games Begin

THE FOLLOWING MORNING, COLLY AND JOSI were met in the lobby of the hotel by Agent Ceca. Josi smiled largely and reached out to shake his hand. Colly politely nodded and glanced over to the big, glass front doors. She instantly noticed the two other agents who stood there watching them.

The three of them walked slowly out to the street and stopped at the edge of the busy sidewalk. Colly sniffed the air, snapped her jaw, and looked at Josi.

"Well, we'll be close, but not too close," Agent Ceca said to the twins. He looked at his watch and smiled coldly. "Do you need anything?"

Colly and Josi looked at him and stayed silent. Andy quickly pulled two small discs out of his suit pocket and gave one to Colly and one to Josi.

"These are tracking devices. I'll be able to follow you two, and if there is trouble, we will be close by," he said.

The twins turned the little discs over in their hands with childlike curiosity and then shoved them in their pockets.

Then, without warning or saying goodbye, they stepped away and began walking down the sidewalk toward Times Square. They walked at a slightly brisk pace and weaved smoothly through the tourists and other obstacles.

"This way, Sis." Colly motioned to Josi as they snapped to the left down a side street.

"Colly, I feel strange," Josi said and grabbed her sister's hand.

"Me too," Colly said and looked left and right. "I know this is weird, but I'm horny."

Josi smiled and pulled Colly along down the tree-lined street. "It's okay; so am I. It must be part of the change. I can sense them, Colly. They don't know they are being tracked. They have no idea."

Colly didn't answer. She was focused on trying to get some kind of location on their prey. She couldn't lock into anything yet.

As the morning sun ticked across the sky, the twins continued to track the trio of fugitives through New York. Each twin waited for that audible click deep in her mind that indicated some kind of hit.

Later that day, just after a quick stop for lunch, the girls paced down Fourth Avenue. Josi stopped, fell against the side of a Starbucks, and gasped.

"Josi! Are you okay?" Colly said as she held her sister up by the arms.

"It's the girl. She's close. Colly, can't you feel that?"

"No, not yet. Which way is she?" Colly looked around nervously.

Josi regained her composure and nodded toward Second Avenue. "She's this way. Focus and you'll feel her. She's … she's scared."

The twins walked quickly toward Second Avenue, weaving and sidestepping in and out of the crowds. They were close, and now both of them could feel it. They each wore a slight grin on their faces as they closed in on their prey.

16

Tiggy is Nervous. On the Run. Who Wants Ice Cream?

TIGGY LEFT THE APARTMENT IN QUEENS AND solemnly made her way into Manhattan. An hour earlier, both Arch and Jake had had their way with her, and she now felt used and dirty. Her vagina was sore, and she felt like she needed a shower.

While riding the subway into Manhattan, she continued having nagging second thoughts about the choices she had made in her life. Not for the first time today, she considered turning herself in and hoping for mercy from the council on Gliese. Her guilt and regret were weighing on her, and it was becoming almost unbearable.

She wandered into a small boutique store on the corner of Second Avenue and Twentieth Street on the east side of Manhattan. She stuffed a small coral bracelet into her pocket and smiled at the girls working the counter. She continued to walk up and down the aisles and eyed the colorful jewelry and clothes.

She let out a small breath and glanced up from the racks of clothes. She saw Josi and Colly through the big front window. Tiggy froze. Something instinctively clicked deep in her physique, and in an instant flash of terror, she knew who they were, what they were, and why they were here. As a child on Gliese, she had heard tales of a long-extinct race of Gliesen people, Star Warriors. Her brother had told her stories of how they could see into people and move things using their minds. He told her how they were used as the brutal sword of justice. Now, she was face to face with two of them. She had no doubt that they were here for her.

Her blood ran cold, and she barely noticed the small amount of urine that leaked out of her bladder and dampened her panties. She watched, wide-eyed, as the twins scanned the block. Her knees felt like rubber, and her ears began to buzz. The world around her turned gray and she felt sweaty and faint.

"Shit," Tig whimpered under her breath. She turned toward the back of the store and looked at the exit sign above the brightly painted metal door that led out to the alley behind the boutique.

She walked as casually as she could toward the back of the store, pushed the door open, and jogged down the alley. She desperately trying to keep the panic at bay; all she wanted to do was put as much distance between her and the strange twins as she could.

"Go. Go. Go. C'mon, Tiggy. Keep it together, girl. Get your ass back to the apartment and figure out your next move," she panic-mumbled to herself.

She peeked out onto Second Avenue from the alley and nonchalantly began a light trot. She looked back over her shoulder as she picked up her pace.

In front of the store, the Geminis looked at each other with raised eyebrows. The city buzzed and moved all around them. A fire truck roared by with sirens and lights blazing, while throngs of people walked around them. Despite the urban noise and chaos, they were honing in on their prey.

"Did you feel that?" Josi asked.

"Uh-huh. She saw us," Colly said and looked around. "Come on, Josi. This way," she said as she looked down Second Avenue.

The twins were now on the hunt, resembling two exotic wildcats on the prowl. As they moved down Second Avenue, past Nineteenth Street, their heads moved slowly from side to side as their long legs moved in a strange stealth pattern down the sidewalk. They lurched and moved in a curious, almost sexual fashion. A young boy, clad in an "I Love NY" T-shirt, watched with his mouth open as he compared the two in his mind to the velociraptors he saw in his dinosaur books and TV shows.

Several onlookers were awestruck as they watched the girls make their way quickly down the sidewalk. Many pedestrians moved out of their way as the twins bounced down Second Avenue, their faces blank and focused.

The girls could smell Tiggy as she walked quickly, tripping over her own feet and constantly turning and looking behind her. She emitted a small whining noise as she ran into people and looked for some kind of escape.

Josi thought to her sister: *Colly, she's afraid.*

Colly pushed her head forward and snapped her jaw. *I know, Josi-girl. She's ahead of us, I think. Can you feel her?*

Josi didn't answer. In an instant, following some strange internal instinct, the twins' quick walk turned into a light jog and then a sprint as they saw Tiggy trying to cross Second Avenue. They accelerated their sprint; their long legs covered an amazing amount of asphalt. They leapt over taxi hoods as their heads stayed locked on their prey like a pair of lionesses.

Tiggy trotted across Second Avenue. Tears streamed down her face and snot ran out of her nose. She turned and saw them coming like something out of her nightmares. She tried running faster, but it was pointless, and she knew it. Josi leaped over a row of Citi Bikes and snapped to the right, cutting her off. Just as she turned to avoid Josi, Colly pounced on her with amazing ferocity. She leapt full force and caught Tiggy with her shoulder directly on her hips, jerking her off her feet. Colly hit her with such force that Tiggy's shoes came off as she flew through the air and smashed through the glass front window of an ice-cream shop.

The sound of breaking glass and the screams of bystanders shattered the mundane city noise. Hours later, as the local police took reports from witnesses, one observer stated that it was like watching one of the New York Jets' front linemen hitting a teenage girl.

Out of breath, both girls stood in front of the demolished front window and looked down at the outlaw, Tiggy. She had a compound fracture of her right arm, and copious amounts of blood came from the countless cuts made by the glass window. She had smashed through the front window and landed on the big, glass ice-cream cooler. Mountains of ice-cream cones, napkins, and little plastic spoons were all over the floor and Tig. Small, red pools of blood seemed to be everywhere.

"Holy shit, is she alive?" Colly asked. She looked down at Tig and then around at the growing crowd.

As if on cue, Tiggy moaned and shifted to her side. She yelped and began to cry as she inadvertently put pressure on the bone that was sticking out through the skin of her arm. The owner of the ice-cream shop ran out from the back room, holding a broom. He skidded to a stop, looked at Tig, then out at the twins in utter shock and surprise.

"Jesus Christ ... call an ambulance," he whispered, wide-eyed.

"I guess that answers that," Josi said with a twisted smile.

The pair slowly slipped away from the huge crowd that had gathered. Then, as discreetly as possible, they made their way back up Second Avenue toward the Plaza Hotel.

Within minutes, Agent Ceca and three other agents showed up and escorted Tiggy in an ambulance to Mount Sinai Hospital. Four days later, a battered and bandaged Tiggy was in cuffs, sitting in a small conference room at Area 51. Her body still ached, and her crotch was bandaged up with something that felt like a diaper. She waited nervously for the Gliesen Guard to arrive and return her to Gliese, where she would be executed by firing squad some fourteen days later.

17

A Simple Plan

EARLY THE NEXT MORNING, JOSI AND COLLY sat on a bench in Central Park, drinking their fancy coffee. The day was pleasant and warm, and the girls were both in a good mood after yesterday's success.

"So, one down and two to go, Sis," Colly said and craned her neck toward the sun.

Josi nodded and mimicked her sister looking into the sun.

"The sun feels different to me than it did a few years ago. It feels, I don't know … dirtier?" Josi said questioningly.

Colly silently agreed.

"So, what's the plan for today?" Colly said with a little laugh.

"You know, I was thinking about the obvious. We can spend the day walking around the city, trying to get a lock on one of them, or we can just go ask Tiggy where her friends are," Josi said rather plainly.

"That simple, Sis? As soon as she sees us, she is going to cloud her mind. She knows what we are, and she might be ready for us," Colly said as she bent forward to tighten up her shoelaces. "Besides, she may not know where they are, and by now, they may have guessed that Tiggy is caught. I mean … who knows what's going on."

"Oh, you can persuade her, I'm sure," Josi said and shot her sister a mischievous grin.

"Fine. I guess it's worth a shot," Colly said as she watched a group of young men jog by, puffing out their chests in some strange form of vanity.

Josi giggled and nudged Colly as the group of guys stumbled as they looked at the sisters.

"Let's go visit our little friend in the hospital and get this shit done," Colly said and stood up.

An hour later, the twins walked into Mount Sinai Hospital and made their way up to the Seventh floor.

18

Zombie. Wallis Wants Answers. Tiggy's Vagina

THE ELEVATOR DOOR OPENED AND JOSI AND Colly stepped out. They looked right and then left. Down the hall was the busy nurses' station, buzzing like a hive of chatty bees. The pair walked right by without saying a word, despite the nurses' calls of, "Can I help you?"

They approached the room that was easily identified as where the fugitive Tiggy was being held, red-flagged by the two police officers sitting on stools by the door. The two officers stood up as the girls approached.

"Can we help you?" The alpha officer said with his chest pumped up.

Colly held up her index finger and wiggled it back and forth, inches from the officer's nose. Both officers sat down and looked straight ahead.

"Neat trick," Josi said and smiled.

Colly smiled back at her sister. "Been working on that one, Sis. Always remember, a soft mind can be extremely palatable in most cases."

Josi nodded and looked down at the officers, who sat in a zombie-like state.

"But are they okay?"

Colly shrugged. "Yeah, they'll be fine in an hour."

Just as the girls were opening the door to go see Tiggy, Colly stopped, lifted the alpha officer's hand, and dropped it on the other officer's crotch. She then did the same thing to the other constable.

The girls burst out laughing in adolescent immaturity. Colly pushed Josi into the room, where Tiggy was secured with restraints to the bed. They needed to have a little chat.

Tiggy let out a small moan of surprise and fear as the door opened and the smiling twins walked in. She looked past the girls to see where the police officers were. Then, in an instant, panic began swelling up in her. She gave the restraints a little tug in a vain attempt to get her arms free.

"How are you feeling?" Josi asked her sympathetically as she sat down in a chair by the window.

She sniffed and glared at the girls. Her arm was in a cast, and she had stitches all over the upper part of her body. Her eyes were blackened, and she was missing her front teeth.

"How the fuck do you think I feel?" she snapped. Her voice was lispy and strained from her front teeth being knocked out.

"Well, you look like shit," Colly remarked vividly and sat down on the corner of her bed.

Colly looked her up and down. "Listen, Tiggy, let's cut to the bullshit. We are going to ask you one question, just one. Answer us, and I promise we will leave. You need to think long and hard about your choice to answer or to stay quiet."

Tiggy looked over at Josi, who sat in the chair. Josi nodded sympathetically and smiled. Tig turned back to Colly, narrowed her eyes, and stared.

Tiggy started to count in her head. *1, 2, 3, 4.* She thought about flowers and dogs. Birds and bees. Limericks danced in her head as she did her best to cloud her mind. She knew she needed to block the twins from getting into her head. If her mind opened, she knew this strange girl would feel answers that she didn't want to give.

Colly stood up and leaned into Tiggy. The tip of her nose just barely touched Tiggy's. They were literally nose to nose.

"Tell me, where are your friends?" Colly whispered in a childlike version of sensuality.

"Go. Fuck. Your. Self," Tiggy whispered hoarsely back and smiled.

Before Tiggy could say another word, Colly stood up straight and yanked the sheets off the bed in a quick pull. She then carefully opened her hospital gown, humiliating a naked and exposed Tiggy. Josi started to say something but stayed quiet.

Colly took the tips of her fingers and slowly ran them across Tiggy's stomach. She worked her fingers up to her breasts and made little circles around Tiggy's nipples. Finally, she cupped Tiggy's breast and gave a playful squeeze. Colly smiled and took a deep breath.

An instant later, Colly raised her eyebrow to Tiggy, giving her one last chance. Tiggy remained defiantly silent and continued to fill her head with letters and numbers. Colly then punched her in her lady parts, hard. Josi jumped in surprise as Tiggy wailed in pain, thrashing and twisting. Again, Colly punched her crotch, this time putting a hairline fracture in her pelvic bone. Tiggy began sobbing like a child. Finally, Colly grabbed her between the legs and started to twist, pull, and squeeze. She could feel the blood start dripping on her hand and running through her fingers. Josi stared at her sister, wide-eyed and open-mouthed.

"Queens! They are in Queens!" Tiggy screamed through her sobs.

"Where in Queens?" Colly asked calmly and applied more and more pressure to Tiggy's now destroyed vagina.

"Jackson Heights! By the airport! An apartment!" Tiggy turned white and passed out.

Josi stood up and started to walk with Colly in tow. Josi tossed her a small towel she grabbed from Tiggy's nightstand, and Colly wiped her hands and tossed the towel absentmindedly.

"That was easier than I thought," Josi remarked as they opened the door and walked past the two police officers still in their zombie-like state with hands on each other's crotches. Josi laughed again as she looked down at the officers.

"You know ... that is funny as hell," Josi snarked.

As the twins walked past the nurses' station on their way to the elevator banks, Colly nodded at the nurses and said, "You might want to check on the little lady at the end of the hall."

An hour later, the girls were back at the Plaza Hotel eating cold, leftover pizza and planning for the next day.

Later that night, they lay in bed, watching TV and eating popcorn. Colly hit the mute button and looked at her sister.

"Josi, my head hurts."

Josi looked at her sister. "Mine does too. I don't think I can handle hunting down more than one of them a day. It's tough on my Blush."

Colly nodded and held her sister's hand. "One at a time, then."

They returned to their popcorn and campy TV shows, nursing their headaches, while preparing for another day of hunting.

General Wallis sat at his desk with his encrypted phone pressed against his ear. On the other line was Agent Ceca.

"Talk to me. What happened today?" Wallis said as he lit a cigarette.

Andy looked out his window in his Brooklyn apartment. He had an amazing view of the Verrazano-Narrows Bridge. He knew this call was coming, and he had rehearsed what he was going to say.

"Well, there was a little problem at the hospital. They went to see the fugitive and, well … let's just say their approach was less than subtle."

Wallis grunted. "The hospital is not pleased. They are blaming the NYPD. Then, to top it off, they drugged the officers on duty and put their hands on each other's dicks, or something like that."

Andy held back a laugh when he heard that.

"Look, General, there isn't a lot that I can do at this point. I am just doing what I was told to do: stand back and observe," Andy said.

Andy heard Wallace sigh on the other end. "You're right," the general said. "Just keep an eye on them, and let's just hope this gets wrapped up sooner rather than later."

"Yes, sir, General. I'm on it," Andy said confidently and hung up the phone.

19

Jackson Heights. Jake Gets Laid. Splat!

THE FOLLOWING DAY, COLLY AND JOSI STOOD by the glass doors that led into the apartment building that the fugitives had rented. It didn't take them long to find the hideout. Earlier, they had taken the train to Jackson Heights and began pounding the pavement. They were, in short order, able to lock in on the old apartment building.

Josi gave the huge door a few quick tugs. Locked.

"Colly," Josi said and nodded toward the big doors.

Colly looked around and tapped the door handle with her finger several times. "Come on," she whispered, and the door made an audible clicking noise and popped open.

"This way," Josi said as she ducked into the lobby and pulled Colly along.

Across the street from the apartment, Agent Ceca sat in his sedan and watched the girls. He took a deep breath and shook his head. He had been tailing the twins all day, and now they were at this run-of-the-mill apartment complex in Queens. He was still absorbing the idea that he was watching girls from another galaxy hunt down intergalactic fugitives. Not for the first time, he wondered how many people were aware of this operation. He guessed as few as possible. Ten? Maybe twenty? Who knew? You might as well ask how many angels could dance on the head of a pin. No matter, he supposed. His job was clear, and he would do as he was instructed by Wallis and Bonilla.

Once they were inside the mundane, vanilla lobby of the apartment building, Josi looked around, deep in thought. There were piles of junk mail on the floor, and the lobby smelled like old cigarettes. She tasted the air and with certainty said to her sister, "He's on the fifth floor, sweetheart."

They took the stairs instead of the elevator. Josi wasn't sure why her instincts told her to stay out of the elevator, but she listened to her head and trusted it.

"Ugh. Stairs? Come on, Jo-Jo, it's five floors." Colly pouted.

"Race you!" Josi said as she exploded in a sprint up the stairs.

Colly laughed and chased after her sister. They were able to leap four or five stairs with each bound. Colly grabbed onto her sister and tried to pull her back. They laughed and pushed each other up the stairs.

At the fifth-floor door, they each took a deep breath and looked around the stairwell.

"You ready?" Colly asked.

Josi nodded and opened the door to the fifth-floor hallway. They cautiously peeked out into the dirty hallway and looked left and then right. They walked slowly down the hall and lightly touched each door. Eventually, Colly's fingers tingled as she brushed the door that read "5F" on a little brass plate.

"Here," she said quietly to her sister.

In unison, they leaned into the door and listened.

"Oh, shit," Josi said and started to giggle.

From inside the apartment, the sounds of sex could be heard. A woman was moaning loudly and saying the name *Jake* over and over.

"Should we wait until they are finished?" Josi asked.

"I don't know; I guess so," Colly said and giggled.

The twins sat on the floor next to the apartment door and listened to the orchestra of sex coming out of 5F. Colly hummed the song "Red Barchetta" by Rush, and Josi tapped her fingers to the beat.

Colly stopped humming and took a deep breath.

"You know, I'm still a virgin," she said.

Josi smiled. "I know. So am I."

The twins looked at each other and started to laugh. Just then, the noises from the apartment ceased, and the twins held their breath. A brief minute later, the door swung open, and a scantily clad girl stepped out. She walked down the hall and adjusted her garters and stockings. She looked back at the girls and smiled seductively. Josi and Colly leaned forward and watched her walk away with her hips swaying. Just as she stepped into the elevator, she gave the twins a little wave. In unison, the girls waved back.

"Ready?" Colly asked as they stood up.

"Ready," Josi said.

Jake was pulling on his T-shirt when he heard the door creak. He froze in mid-motion and watched the door with his eyes squinted ever so slightly.

"Tiggy? Arch?" he asked nervously as he began to dress quickly while staring at the door.

Suddenly, the door opened, and Josi and Colly stood in the doorframe.

"Oh, shit," Jake said as he buttoned his jeans.

"Hi, Jake," Colly said and looked around the sparsely furnished and unkempt apartment. "Time's up, my friend."

Jake stood tall in a vain attempt to be intimidating.

"Who are you?" Jake asked and brushed the hair out of his face.

"It doesn't matter. What matters is, it's time for you to go home, Jake. Playtime is over," Josi chimed in.

Jake looked the twins up and down. A small grin appeared on his otherwise stony face.

"You're Gliese, aren't you?"

The twins shot him a smile back. "We are. Now take a guess on why we are here on Earth," Josi said as they took a step forward.

Jake knew. Like Tiggy, in an instant, he knew who the girls were and what they wanted. His stomach turned over, and he felt weak. From outside the window, a car drove by with its radio blaring.

Jake took a single step back, and with an explosion of spontaneity, he bolted past the twins and out into the hall.

"Fuck!" Colly screamed as she fell against the wall.

Josi helped her up and they dashed out into the hall. Jake, in his panic, had run the wrong way. He ran away from the elevator and stairs and into the small hall that had a single stairwell that led up to the roof.

"C'mon, Sis. Let's grab him," Josi said and pulled Colly along.

Jake ran up the darkened stairwell to the top of the building and threw open the door. He was immediately blinded by the bright sunlight and shielded his eyes.

"Fuck!" he snapped and looked around.

He was on the roof of the apartment building, and he knew was trapped like an animal. He turned around in circles, looking for some way out. He trotted over to the edge and looked over the side.

"Shit," he mumbled under his breath.

The door that led to the roof was thrown open, and Colly and Josi stepped out. Colly walked slowly toward him while Josi sidestepped and started to hook around to his left. Jake's eyes darted back and forth between the two of them. It was as if they were setting him up for the kill, not unlike wild animals do before they tear into their prey.

"Over the edge, or give up? It's your choice, stupid." Colly mocked him as the twins stepped a little closer and smiled.

Jake knew that no matter what, he was a dead man. If he jumped, he would die. If he gave up, he would die by Gliesen hands, and if he chose to fight, the twins would kill him. His options were bleak.

"Fuck you!" Jake screamed as he backed up to the ledge.

Josi let out a small, comical gasp. "Come on, Jake. Don't be like that," she said, softly mocking him.

"I'll jump! I swear I'll jump!" Jake warned in a high-pitched plea.

The twins looked at each other and then back at Jake. They both stood with their arms crossed.

"Jake, think about this very carefully," Josi said calmly. "You're caught; that's it. Game over, moron."

Jake knew it was game over. In a flash, he thought back to his childhood on Gliese. He remembered standing on a small ledge that stood above a creek in the woods behind his house. All his chums would stand on that ledge and leap out over the creek, rolling as they landed. They laughed and high-fived each other as they made their way back up the hill to jump again and again.

"Come on, Jakey! It's your turn, Jake! It's easy!" they would yell as they clamored up the hill. Despite his pals' words of encouragement, Jake never mustered the courage to jump.

He took a deep breath, smiled, and fell backward over the edge. As he fell, he thought of the creek and his childhood friends. He didn't jump all those years ago, but he did now. In an instant, he made up for all the times he stood there with his hands stuffed in the pockets of his short pants, kicking the stones at his feet and watching his friends jump the creek.

There was a collective gasp from the crowds on the sidewalk as the smiling face of Jake struck the cement with a dull, wet thud.

Out of his peripheral vision, Andy caught the last flash of life before Jake smashed into the sidewalk.

"Fuck!" he said through clenched teeth.

He pushed open the door and immediately ran to the lifeless body. He looked up just in time to see the twins staring over the edge.

"Goddamn," he mumbled under his breath while he pulled out his phone to call 911.

"Whoa," Josi said as she looked over the side and watched the crowd grow around Jake's body. "I didn't see *that* coming!"

"No shit. That's fucked up. He's got balls; I'll give him that. At least we didn't have to beat the shit out of him," Colly chimed in as they stared down over the ledge.

"Two down and one to go," Josi said as the twins turned around and walked away.

They skirted down the stairs and crept out the back door. Two blocks away, they jumped on the subway and began making their way back to Manhattan and the Plaza Hotel. The ride on the subway was solemn, despite the fact that they had eliminated one of the fugitives.

Josi leaned her head on her sister's shoulder and thought to her, *Are you okay?*

Colly closed her eyes and responded silently. *Yeah, yeah. I'm good.*

Fifteen minutes later, the block in front of the apartment was sealed off, and Agent Ceca was on the phone with Wallis, informing him of the death of one of the fugitives. He informed the general that the details were sketchy and the girls were now MIA, but Ceca assumed they were heading back to the Plaza Hotel.

"Find them!" Wallis barked.

The general hung up the phone and quickly dialed the president to inform him of the status of the operation. One of the fugitives was dead, and one was in custody. The president listened carefully and asked the general to keep him posted on any new developments.

20

Andy and Josi.
Colly Shows Her Undies.
The Verrazano Bridge

AN HOUR AFTER LEAVING THE FUGITIVE JAKE'S apartment, Josi and Colly sat in the bar at the Plaza Hotel, sipping drinks and reflecting on their day.

"Well, Sis ... penny for your thoughts?" Josi said.

Colly shrugged and looked around the bar. "I don't know. I feel kind of bad for him."

"Don't," Josi said and took her sister's hand. "You just remember the people he killed on Gliese. Those kids he made fatherless. Remember that. They killed here on Earth, too. You know that. You can feel it just the same as I can."

Colly nodded and sighed. "I know; I know. You're right. They are bad people."

Just then, Josi looked up from her drink and saw Agent Ceca walk into the lounge, looking right and left. Josi gulped and gently kicked Colly under the table.

"What, Josi?" Colly said, irritated.

"It's Andy," Josi said nervously. She tried her best to fix her hair and adjust herself. Andy saw them and gave a wave as he walked toward them.

"Oh, shit, here he comes," Josi said, feeling incredibly nervous and giddy.

"Relax, Sis," Colly said coolly. She looked at her sister and smiled.

Andy walked to the table with confidence.

"Hi, guys. Okay if I sit?"

Both Colly and Josi nodded and smiled. Andy shot a quick look at Josi and smiled lightly.

"So, what happened out there?" he asked, immediately getting down to business.

The twins looked at each other, and Colly asked what seemed obvious to the girls. "Well, weren't you there? I thought you were supposed to be 'close, but not too close.'"

Josi smiled at her sister's passive barb as the waitress walked up and took Andy's order for a club soda.

"I was there," Andy said firmly. "I don't know what happened on that rooftop, but I do know the fire department is hosing down the street in front of the building as we speak."

In unison, Colly and Josi exhaled. Andy sat back in his chair as if he were waiting for some type of grand explanation.

"Andy, it was his choice. He jumped; we didn't throw him off the roof," Colly said, somewhat nonchalantly.

Andy smiled. "Just like you didn't punch the other one in the groin and mutilate her vagina to the point that she could barely walk? Then you guys did something to the officers that were guarding her? You drugged them and put their hands on their dicks, or something like that?"

Colly and Josi held back the giggles. "Oh my God, we didn't drug them!" an exasperated Josi said, in their defense.

Andy shook his head. "Listen, do me a favor and leave the NYP out of your antics. Just nab the last fugitive and let's call it a day, okay?"

The twins smiled and looked slyly at each other. In the end, they agreed to what Andy had said.

After a half hour of light chitchat, Colly stood up and excused herself. She informed Josi and Andy that she was going to head up to the room and get cleaned up. There was a little dress shop around the corner that she wanted to see, and she also wanted to try some of the unusual New York cuisine for dinner. Of course, this was all very well planned by Colly to let her sister spend some alone time with Andy. She peekabooed into her sister just long enough to know she was crushing hard on the FBI agent from Brooklyn.

An hour later, Josi and Andy were walking slowly through Central Park, chatting lightly. They spoke easily and freely to each other. Their guards were dropped, and they quickly discovered that despite Josi living light-years away, they had a great deal in common.

"So, you're a Mets fan, eh?" Josi asked and nudged him.

"Ever since I was a kid. I take it you're a Yankees girl?" Andy replied slickly.

"I am. I guess you can say that first and foremost, I am a baseball fan. There isn't any true baseball on Gliese, so I'm constantly missing my boys from the Bronx. My sister and I went to a game the other day, and we had a blast."

"I bet you guys did!" Andy said, imagining the mischief they must have pulled at Yankee Stadium. "So, tell me, Josi. Tell me about this weird ability you and Colly have to hunt and read into people."

Josi shrugged. "What do you want to know?"

"Well, what's it called?" Andy asked.

"Well, it's technically called Blush," Josi said. "Or as Colly and I call it, peekaboo. Most people on Gliese think it's just a legend, or a parlor trick or something. Like on Earth, how some people claim to be able to talk to the dead or see the future and some people believe it. It's kinda like that, I suppose."

"Only it's not a parlor trick, is it?" Andy said and smiled.

"No, not for me and Colly, it's not. One time, Colly told me we were Star Children, but ... I don't know." Josi stopped and looked at Andy. "It's like standing outside of the library. If you go in, you can have the answers to anything you want to know. All you have to do is pick up the book and read. To my sister and I, people are books. If we choose to, we can pull them off the shelf and simply read. I guess I'm oversimplifying it a little, but that's the gist of it."

They started to walk again, and Josi continued, "Oddly enough, I sometimes have a hard time with my Blush on Gliese. Colly thinks it's because I spent so many years on Earth, but I notice she has hiccups with hers on Earth. I've also noticed it … it stalls sometimes. Like a computer that freezes and you need to unplug it and reboot. My sister says it's just part of the Blush that needs to grow, but I'm not sure."

Andy smiled and said, "I like you, Josi Andolini."

Josi smiled and bit her lip. "I like you, too. I just hope you're okay with long distance relationships."

They both laughed, and they held hands.

They walked through the park, and their conversation carried on and on. Andy told Josi about his job at the FBI, and Josi painted him a visual picture of her life on Gliese. She told him about how Colly had found her and took her back home to Gliese. She told him about her job as a teacher and how she lived on the ocean and all about the clean solar winds that blew across her balcony at night. Andy listened with astonishment and awe as she rambled on and on.

"So, how do you manage the technology to travel through space?" Andy laughed. His curiosity was getting the best of him.

Josi shrugged. "Honestly, I don't really get how it works. It's like asking someone how a text message gets sent; it just does. I do know that it isn't really about distance. You know, miles … it's about time and the ability to bend and fold it. I know that really doesn't answer your question, but it's the best I can do."

Andy smiled. "Well, it's an amazing thing, don't you agree?"

"Oh, it definitely is. When I first got home to Gliese, I was constantly astounded at the technology they have," Josi said and looked at Andy.

"So," Josi said, changing the subject. "You live in Bay Ridge?"

Andy nodded. "Yep. I have an amazing view of the Verrazano Bridge."

Josi bit her lip. "I'd love to see that!"

Twenty minutes later, they were in Andy's government-issued sedan, driving over the Brooklyn Bridge on their way to Bay Ridge.

"Do you have this in blue?" Colly asked the somewhat snarky clerk in the boutique she'd stopped in as she dress shopped along Madison Avenue.

"We do," the clerk said with a hint of a smile on his face.

"Can I see it in blue? Size two." Colly excitedly clapped her hands.

The clerk excused himself and walked quickly to the back of the store while Colly walked around the front of the store and looked at the pretty clothes. A handful of customers in the store were secretly watching her, some of them smiling and clandestinely trying to get close to her.

"Here you go, blue in a size two," the clerk said as she handed Colly the short dress.

Colly trotted off to the dressing room to try on the dress. A quick minute later, she stepped out to look at herself in the big mirror.

"So. What do you think?" she asked the clerk and several of the well-to-do female patrons in the store.

"It's lovely," the clerk said, with a hint of reserved dismay in his voice.

Colly started spinning and laughing, and the dress flared up and up and up. Eventually, she spun around so that her pink underwear was clearly visible to everyone in the store. Most of the well-to-do women laughed and covered their mouths.

"I'll take it!" She hooted.

She didn't bat an eye at the $2,000 price tag on the Cavalli dress as she handed the clerk the same American Express she used two years earlier while in New York. The clerk ran the card, packaged the dress carefully in the red-and-white box, and handed it to Colly.

"Come again," he said and smiled as Colly scooted out the door.

Colly walked back to the hotel, got her face dolled up, changed into her new dress, and headed out for a bite to eat. As she climbed into the cab, she tried calling her sister in her head. No response. Colly wrinkled her lip and closed her eyes tightly.

The cab driver kept stealing glances at Colly in the rearview mirror. Finally, Colly barked out, "What?"

The cabbie quickly looked down, and Colly smiled and giggled to herself. As she left the cab, she handed the cabbie a small roll of twenty-dollar bills and told him to have a great night.

The ultra-trendy restaurant was crowded, but Colly was immediately seated at the bar while her table for one was prepared. From across the room, a man in a business suit walked over and leaned against the bar close to Colly.

"If you aren't waiting for someone, we would love to have you join our little group," he said and motioned toward his table of coworkers.

Colly looked over at the table of five businessmen, who looked like they were all cut from the same cloth. In unison, they all waved at her.

"Oh, well, sure," Colly said and smiled.

At the table, the men all introduced themselves one at a time. Steve, Mike, Mike, Robert, Donny, and Josh. Colly politely shook each one's hand and made it known that she was very happy to have met each one.

The waitress came over and replaced all their drinks and handed Colly a Grape Crush. She gave Colly a little wink and a smile. Colly winked back seductively.

One of the Mikes leaned toward Colly and asked nervously, "So, what's your name, and what's a nice girl like you doing in a place like this?"

His colleagues rolled their eyes at his cheesy opening line. Nevertheless, they all turned toward Colly to see what she might say.

Colly held up her finger as she swallowed a big gulp of Crush and said, most casually, "Well, my name is Colly, and I live on the planet Gliese. It's about twenty light-years from here, and it's very beautiful. I'm here on Earth with my sister, Josi. We were sent here on an assignment to hunt down three fugitives from our planet that are hiding out on Earth."

Colly took another sip from her Grape Crush and continued matter-of-factly. "Two years ago, I stole an orb. Well, I actually kinda borrowed it from this space pirate named Fietch and came here to get my sister. I got sprayed by a skunk and wrecked a Jaguar F-type into a hair salon. Got into a little trouble with that mishap. What about you guys? What do you do?"

No one said anything. The men sat in silence, mouths agape. Finally, one of the Mikes spoke up. "Ahhhh ... well, we all work down on Wall Street, but that doesn't sound nearly as exciting as what you do."

Colly nodded and smiled softly. "You better believe that, lollipop!"

The rest of the evening was full of surprises from Colly. She kept the small group of soon-to-be Wall Street tycoons in a constant trance of comical escapades that made them laugh hysterically.

Unbeknownst to the young professionals, her Blush was working overtime as she peeked quickly into each guy, one at a time. More than once, she chided herself for doing so.

She quickly discovered that the excessively arrogant man, Josh, who told Colly he was single, actually had a wife and two young sons at home. The young man, Steve, who seemed to be the quietest of the group, was stealing money from his clients and just bought a boat with his ill-gotten loot. And the well-built guy, Robert, was in fact a warm-hearted man who secretly hated his friends and their Wall Street lifestyle. Colly smiled as she read his wish to bicycle across America.

As the night spun out and the minutes ticked by, Colly finally excused herself to use the bathroom and quietly slipped out without saying goodbye. She was getting bored and restless and felt like moving.

Before she left, she handed the waitress a little wad of folded one-hundred-dollar bills to pay for everyone's meals and drinks. She squeezed the pretty waitress's hand lightly and Blushed her. Gently and slowly, she leaned in and blew a sweet breath into her ear, then stepped back and stared. The waitress gasped a little and smiled. Colly swung her hips around and sauntered out the door.

Colly bounced out onto Seventh Avenue and stood on the curb with her hand in the air. A quick cab ride later, she was back at the Plaza. She had hoped Josi would be at the hotel watching TV or eating pizza, but she was still missing.

Josi and Andy sat comfortably on the balcony, sipping wine and chatting lightly. The view of the Verrazano Bridge was exactly as Andy had described, and the wine was making Josi feel giddy and childlike.

"Well, you certainly weren't kidding about the view. Did you grow up here, in Bay Ridge?" Josi asked while taking small sips of the wine.

"I did. My folks are long gone, but I grew up not too far from here," Andy said.

Josi nodded. "I spent my childhood in Hell's Kitchen, and then when my parents died, I bought a place just around the corner. At the time, I couldn't see living anywhere else in the world."

Andy began to chuckle softly.

"What's so funny?" Josi asked.

"You live a very long way from Hell's Kitchen now." Andy poked fun as he sat up from his chair and looked up into the inky-black sky.

He held out his hand to help Josi up and then looked back into the night sky. "Which one is yours?" he asked, motioning to the sky.

Josi smiled and pointed to a faint and distant star. "That's it; that's home."

They went into the apartment and poured a little more wine for Andy. Josi declined the refill and leaned against the counter. Against her better judgment, she looked into Andy quickly. She felt kindness and warmth. He was the one. She just knew.

She took his hand and pulled him close. Her lips met his, and Andy dropped his glass on the floor. They clumsily made their way to the bedroom, kissing and pulling off each other's clothes. He threw her on the bed and kissed her deeply. His hand found her breasts, and Josi let out a little moan.

Just as he put himself deep into her, her Blush saw bliss. Everything about him indicated benevolence. She moaned and shook as her orgasm flooded through her hips. Her entire mind exploded with color and joy. With every pulse in her hips, her Blush pushed and wrapped itself around her inner psyche. A new piece of this strange puzzle seemed to be implanted into her Blush—a new piece that had been missing and void.

Josi stared at the ceiling and smiled while her breath came out in small, deliberate gasps. Andy's weight felt warm and comforting on her. He kissed her softly, and Josi smiled. Her Blush was almost complete.

About the same time Josi was drinking wine and looking at the Verrazano Bridge, Colly sat on the edge of the bed and waited for her sister to get back to the hotel. She wore Josi's Rolling Stones T-shirt and a pair of sweats. She had just opened a container of mint chocolate chip ice cream and was digging in. With a spoon in one hand and the remote in the other, she settled for watching reruns of *Seinfeld* and laughing hysterically.

Twenty minutes later, Colly froze. Her ice cream fell on the floor, and she closed her eyes tightly with her mouth hanging open.

She smiled and whispered, "Oh. My. Fuck. Josi."

21

Big Surprise

COLLY STOOD BY THE DOOR WITH HER ARMS crossed. She pounced on her sister as soon as she walked in the door, grabbing her by her shoulders and pushing her against the wall.

"Colly! What the fuck?" Josi said and giggled.

"Shhh!" Colly said as she touched her nose against her sister's and slowly made little Eskimo circles.

Josi sighed, rolled her eyes, and stood still while her sister went through the ancient Star Child routine.

"Okay, that's enough!" Josi barked after a few quick seconds.

Colly stepped back and giggled. "Josi-girl!"

Josi laughed and screamed. They ran into the living room of the suite and jumped on the couch.

"Tell me everything!" Colly screamed as they jumped up and down.

"Colly! He's so amazing! He's perfect! He's funny and charming and he loves baseball and he's so handsome and he's such a good kisser! Colly, my Blush exploded!"

"Oh, Josi! I'm so happy for you!" Colly said.

Josi beamed as she dished about Andy. She gave her sister a play-by-play account of the activities of the evening. She told Colly about the view of the bridge and his really cool apartment and how he, too, had a baseball-card collection. Colly hugged her sister and told her how happy she was for her.

Later that night, they lay in bed together, and Colly turned toward Josi.

"Did it hurt? You know … sex?" Colly asked.

"Not as bad as I thought it would," Josi said and smiled with her eyes closed.

Colly grinned and kissed her sister's forehead. "Nighty night, Gemini."

22

Frustration.
The Pittsburgh Pirates

FOR THE NEXT TWO DAYS, THE TWINS SCOURED the city searching for the final, elusive fugitive, Arch. Their search was proving to be maddeningly fruitless and frustrating. On just one occasion, Colly got a hit. They were on the Manhattan Bridge walking into Brooklyn, and Colly stopped in her tracks. She grabbed her sister's hand and turned around, back toward Manhattan.

"Come on, Josi!" she yelled and pulled her twin along.

By the time they got to the end of the bridge, the hit had vanished, and Colly was blank again.

"Shit," Colly mumbled in frustration at her inability to hone in on the prey.

"It's okay, Colly. We'll find him," Josi said reassuringly.

Something seemed to pull Josi toward Chinatown. It wasn't a specific feeling, but perhaps just an urge. After several hours of slowly and methodically scanning the streets of Chinatown, they turned north and headed back uptown.

Had the girls not been so focused on Arch, they would have certainly picked up on Andy and a small group of agents clandestinely following them. Andy was keeping a close eye on Josi, of course. He wasn't sure what type of a criminal Arch could be, but despite the parameters laid down by Wallis, if Josi was in trouble, he was going to step in.

As evening settled in, the twins sat at a small pizzeria on Eighth Avenue to eat a late supper. The girls were quiet and slightly off-balance after the events of the day. Josi gazed out the window and watched the sun set, cutting slices of shadows across the streets.

"Is it possible he left the city?" she asked and folded her slice in half.

"No," Colly said with finality. She watched her sister fold her slice in half and then imitated her the best she could. "I'm not sure why I know, but I know he's still here. He's just being careful, clever, and crafty. Can't you feel it, Josi?"

"No, not really," Josi said and picked absentmindedly at her slice.

Colly sighed and sipped her Grape Crush. She looked at her sister and wondered if everything with Andy was clouding her ability to hunt. She instantly dismissed the thought. Josi would never let anything distract her on such an important task—not even Andy and her newfound attraction for him.

She sighed and noticed of a group of younger girls a few tables over who were staring and taking discreet pictures with their cell phones. Under normal circumstances, Colly would have turned on her silliness and had a ball with them. Not tonight, though. Tonight, her mood was dark and frustrated. Her inability to finish this was something like an itch that she was unable to scratch.

Later that evening, they climbed into bed, and Colly started flipping through the channels on the TV.

"Anything in particular you want to watch?" she asked Josi.

Josi sighed and flipped her pillow over. "I'm crazy about Andy. All I do is think about him," she said dreamily.

Colly smiled. "I know you are, Sis. He seems like a great guy."

"Colly." Josi sighed. "What if I wanted to bring him home? Or, what if I wanted to stay here with him?"

Surprised, Colly looked at her sister and smiled. "Josi, you can do whatever you want. Can you bring him home? Would they let you?"

"I'm not sure. Who would I even ask?" Josi said and chuckled.

"Well, for starters, did you ask Andy about all this?" Colly said.

"No, not really. I mean … what am I supposed to say? 'Andy, do you want to come home with me to another planet?'"

Both girls started laughing. Josi leaned over and gave her sister a quick kiss on the forehead and turned over to go to sleep. Colly spent the next hour or so watching the Pittsburgh Pirates beat up on the Dodgers.

23

Into the Subway. 9mm. My Sister Loves You

ON DAY TWO OF THE HUNT, THE SAME RESULTS seemed to play out yet again. All morning and into the afternoon, the girls were unable to lock in on Arch. The sisters were getting short with each other and shooting irritated looks of frustration back and forth. They had been hunting nonstop, and both had headaches and sore feet. At one point, they rode the elevator to the top of a luxury apartment building and peered out off the roof. They scanned the city and the boroughs from atop the high rise. Nothing.

Then, just before dinner, the girls turned the corner on Twenty-Third Street, and they both stopped in their tracks. The crowd of people behind them had to stop short, and they scowled at them. They both smiled and looked at each other. They knew they had him.

Josi exhaled deeply, and Colly's shoulders seemed to roll back off her joints. Without speaking, they began to slowly walk down Twenty-Third. They stopped at the top of the subway steps and looked down. Josi looked around and caught a glimpse of Andy standing behind them down the block. She waved her pinky finger, and Andy smiled.

They worked their way down the stairs into the subway. As they trotted down, Colly remarked, "Andy is behind us. Can you feel him?"

Josi laughed. "Oh, yeah, I can feel him."

The girls grinned slyly and began to separate from each other. Colly went toward the tracks, while Josi slowly walked along the wall by the bathrooms. Their eyes scanned the crowds slowly. The hundreds of people that moved in angular masses through the station had no idea that these two strange-looking women were, in fact, intergalactic hunters looking for a most dangerous man.

The twins positioned themselves in the station and waited. He was coming. Oh, yes, he certainly was.

As the girls trotted down the stairs into the subway, Andy was close behind. He had instructed his fellow agents to stay up on the street. He didn't want too many people around the twins. He held back just far enough to watch them hunt but not interfere. By now, he was incredibly curious to watch how they would handle this.

As he stood out of the line of sight of the twins, he pulled out his cell phone and began to dial.

"Wallis," the voice on the other end of the line answered.

"General Wallis, this is Agent Ceca."

"Ceca. Where are you?" Wallis snapped.

"I'm in the subway station on Twenty-Third Street. They seem to have a fix on him, but I can't be sure."

Wallis, who was at FBI Headquarters in Manhattan, excused himself from the meeting he was sitting in on and stepped into the hall.

"Everything look like it's under control?" he asked firmly.

"For now, yes. But there's a lot of civilians around. I'm a little worried about that," Andy replied as he scanned the large crowds.

"Can you get to them? See if there's another way?" Wallis asked.

Andy sighed. "I seriously doubt it. They are locked in, and besides, they spent the last two days looking. What if they lose him and can't get to him again?"

"I want constant updates, Ceca," Wallis said and then hung up abruptly.

Andy kept his phone in his hand and pretended to be texting in an attempt to blend in with the crowd and still be able to watch them.

Just as Andy was getting ready to call Wallis and tell him that the status quo was happening, he noticed Josi step away from the wall and slowly walk toward Colly. The sound of the approaching train was growing louder. From Andy's position, he could see the headlight of the train growing bigger and brighter. He realized that the girls had sensed Arch was on that train.

The twins positioned themselves on both ends of the platform, ready to pounce on Arch. The train was getting closer. They were ready.

Inside the crowded train, Arch was nervous and sweating. He knew Jake was dead, and Tiggy was missing and he assumed she was dead, but he didn't know that for sure. Now, not for the first time that day, he pondered the thought that someone from Gliese was here on Earth to capture or kill them. He had figured that the authorities on Gliese knew they had skipped the planet and might be on Earth. He wasn't sure how they were able to figure out they went to New York as opposed to Tokyo, Paris, or Moscow. It didn't matter, he supposed. What mattered was that he needed to reevaluate what was happening and come up with another plan.

The robotic voice on the train announced the Twenty-Third Street station was approaching, and Arch prepared to get off. With his hands stuffed into his pockets, he stood up and felt the cold steel of his newly purchased 9mm gun in his front pocket. He stood by the door and waited for the train to come to a complete stop. The doors swished open and Arch stepped out and looked right and left.

Colly looked down the platform and saw Arch for the first time. She hunched over slightly and snapped her jaw. Her sister made a strange, audible clicking noise, almost as if she was fine-tuning her Blush with her sister, trying to get into perfect sync with her.

Josi stood on the far end of the ramp and lowered herself onto her haunches. More than one person glanced at her and moved on.

The train quickly pulled away, and Arch stood solo on the edge of the platform. In a flash, Arch's world went into slow motion. He instantly saw Josi and gasped. It was as if everything was buzzing around him. His hand instinctively went for the 9mm in his pocket, and he drew the weapon and pointed it at Josi.

Andy dropped his cell phone, yanked his gun from his holster, and screamed, "Josi! Gun!"

Startled, Arch turned toward Andy and fired a single shot. The bullet caught Andy just above the hip bone. He grimaced in pain and crumpled to the ground. His gun dropped onto the tracks, but he didn't notice or care. The throngs of people that filled the platform screamed and ran for cover. Several of the bystanders immediately dropped to the ground and covered their heads.

At that instant, the girls exploded in different directions. Josi leaped toward Andy in a desperate panic; Colly went after Arch.

"Oh my God, Andy!" Josi screamed as she slid on her knees to him. "No! No! No!"

Josi wailed as she cradled him on the dirty ground. She put her hand on the wound to try to stop the bleeding.

Colly, in just two bounding steps, got to Arch just as he was getting ready to shoot again. Colly didn't swat the gun from his hand but rather punched it out from his grip. Arch gasped as Colly grabbed his throat, lifted the little gangster off the ground, and held him up. It was an eerie reflection of how her sister had taken Bobby Underwood two years earlier.

The noise on the platform was deafening. People screamed and pushed as they tried to get to the stairs that led out of the station and to the street above. Suddenly, the Brooklyn-bound express train was roaring down the tracks toward the station. The sound of the train was getting louder as Colly took one step forward and dangled Arch over the tracks by his neck. He kicked his legs and tried to shake loose, to no avail.

Josi looked up and Blushed her sister. *Colly, wait! Just wait!* The seconds spun out as the noise from the train became deafening to the girls.

Now, Colly! Now!

In that split second, with a quick snap of her arm, Colly tossed Arch in front of the speeding express train. He landed on the tracks and screamed as he tried to crawl away—but he was too late. The train hit him and slammed him against the cement pillar next to the tracks, but not before the big steel wheels took off his legs.

Colly looked down triumphantly at Arch as he drew his last breath and died. She snapped her jaw lightly, raised her eyebrows, and ran to her sister, who was still cradling Andy in her arms.

Three agents from Andy's team bolted down the stairs and pushed through the throngs of screaming pedestrians who were making their way up to the street. With guns drawn, they circled Andy and the sisters. In short order, Andy was in the back of an ambulance heading to the hospital, with Josi at his side.

Later that night, the girls sat in Andy's room at Mount Sinai Hospital. Both General Wallis and Bonilla had stopped in and taken statements from the twins and Andy. They nodded and listened intently as Josi and Colly ran a synopsis of what happened to all three of the fugitives. Bonilla jotted down notes and said he would forward all the information to the authorities on Gliese.

The bullet from Arch's 9mm missed Andy's vital organs and went clean through—a lucky break for Andy. He would be in the hospital for a few days, but he would make a full recovery. Josi announced that she wouldn't leave Earth until Andy was out of the hospital. Colly nodded and agreed with her sister.

"Do you want me to get you some ice cream?" Josi asked as she stroked Andy's hair.

"Yes, please," Colly said absentmindedly as she looked out the window.

"Not you, silly!" Josi said and laughed. "Andy? Ice cream?"

"Sure, baby. Get some for Tweedle Dee over there," he said, ribbing Colly.

Josi kissed Andy's forehead and went to get ice cream. Colly sighed and turned to Andy, making sure Josi was out of earshot.

"My sister, she loves you."

"I love her, too. She's like no other woman I've ever met," Andy said.

Colly smiled softly. "She is one of a kind … well, kinda."

"You don't need to worry, Colly. I'll take care of her. Here, Gliese … wherever things end up, I'll take care of her."

Colly smiled and teared up. "She's my Gemini, Andy. I know that you will."

24

Saying Goodbye.
One Last Favor

A WEEK LATER, AT EDWARDS AIR FORCE BASE
in California, Colly and Josi stood by their orb and shook hands with
General Wallis. The sun was warm, and the sky was as blue as one can
imagine.

Colly looked up and smiled. "Your planet is beautiful."

General Wallis nodded and smiled. He was flanked by seven or
eight scientists and government officials, including Lieutenant Bonilla
and some of the joint chiefs. They all came to see the girls off. Standing
in front of the pack was Andy. His side was bandaged, but he was no
worse for wear. Josi hung lightly on his arm; they had already said their
goodbyes in private.

Josi gave Andy a quick kiss on the cheek. "See you soon, right?"

Andy smiled. "See you soon."

Just as the twins were getting ready to step into the orb, Bonilla
stepped forward with a manila folder.

"Girls, just a quick second," Bonilla said, almost reluctantly.

Wallis took a deep breath and asked for the small group of officials
to step away. Andy squeezed Josi's hand and walked back toward the
hangar with the others.

As soon as the group had walked away, Bonilla opened the folder
and handed Colly a single piece of paper. On the paper was a long,
coded message written in loopy, childish handwriting. It was taken
from the evidence locker at police headquarters in Pittsburgh and sent

to the FBI, who passed it along to Wallis in the hopes that he would have luck deciphering it.

Colly looked at it for a long moment, and then Josi impatiently pulled it from her sister's hands and looked at the code.

"Can you tell us anything about this?" Wallis asked.

The girls glanced at each other with raised eyebrows, and Josi asked, "Where did this come from?"

Bonilla shook his head and cleared his throat. "Pittsburgh. Our agents are having a real problem with this, and we were just hoping you could nudge us in the right direction. We are aware this one is not your problem, but perhaps you would consider helping us."

Colly took the piece of paper back from Josi and looked again at the strange code. She sighed and looked at her sister and then at General Wallis.

"Tell the Pittsburgh police to watch the school buses along Forbes Avenue. He's waiting patiently, but his patience is growing thin."

Without saying a word, Bonilla took the coded paper and quickly walked away to a waiting Jeep that sped away. Colly and Josi raised their eyebrows at one another and shrugged.

"Well, General, I guess we could speak soon, eh?" Josi said.

"Have a good trip, girls, and thank you," Wallis said and stepped away from the orb.

Colly pushed and smacked Josi's butt to get her in the small cockpit.

"Stop it, Colly!" Josi snapped.

Colly giggled and slid in the orb. The hatch closed, and with a flash of white light, the orb was gone.

Wallis stood with his hands on his hips and looked into the blue sky. He watched as a small corner of blue wrinkled and folded as the orb bent time and headed home.

Epilogue

Two months after returning to Gliese, the twins walked along the pristine beach, clad in flowing tops and loose beach pants. Sometimes, they would hold hands or walk arm in arm, happy for the peace being together brought.

Josi stopped and faced the waves while the solar wind made her hair dance and spin. The surf boomed and rumbled as shooting stars crisscrossed the early morning sky. Colly stood next to her, looking out into the sea.

"Colly, I'm pregnant," Josi said and smiled.

Colly bit her lip and covered her mouth. The wind continued to blow her long, black hair into her face. She brushed it away and stepped close to her sister. She lifted Josi's chin, just slightly, and gently put her nose on her sister's. She made three tiny circles and stepped back.

"You certainly are pregnant," she said softly. "Have you told Andy?"

"Not yet. I'm going to soon. I have to soon," Josi said.

Colly squared herself up with her sister and placed her fingertips on Josi's still-flat stomach. She closed her eyes as her fingers gently caressed Josi's stomach.

"Josi, she's a Star Child," Colly said excitedly.

"I know," Josi said quietly as the tears welled up in her eyes. "I will name her Calista, after her grandmother, after our mother."

Colly began to cry. She hugged her sister and whispered in her ear, "Josi, we are not the last."

Josi broke away from Colly's hug and softly held her sister's face with both her hands.

"No, Gemini. We are not."

The End.